Dead Dogs & Splintered Hearts

Tom Ward

CROOKED
CAT

Tweet a photo of yourself holding
this book to @crookedcatbooks
and something nice will happen.

For Robert Newlands Isbister

The Author

Tom Ward's first novel A Departure was shortlisted for the People's Book Prize 2014 and the Beryl Bainbridge Award 2014.

He has written journalism for Esquire, Men's Health, The Guardian, GQ, Vice, Marie Claire, Wired and others.

He is also the recipient of the GQ Norman Mailer Award 2012 and can be found on Twitter at @TomWardWrites.

Acknowledgements

With thanks to Shia LaBeouf.

Dead Dogs & Splintered Hearts

A Walk In The Park

"So they said, 'Come back in a week and we'll see if we can take you back'. It's bullshit though. All bullshit, like I said. I said to them, 'Look, there's no way I said what she claims I said.' How do I know what...? Thanks... Yeah, how do I know what she thinks she heard me say? I said to them, I said, 'Look, I'm not one to go around slagging people off, especially not a woman, and especially not at work.' You know that better than anyone, Spence."

"Yup," Spence replied around a mouthful of beer.

"Anyway, it's their loss, isn't it? Here I am with a week off work, the sun shining and all the beers we can drink. So who's laughing now?"

Spence fell silent, drinking quickly from the can before the beer became too warm.

"I'm laughing now," Tony said to himself as he brought his own drink to his lips."

Spence finished his can, crushed it in one hand and threw it off into a bush.

Tony downed his beer and followed Spence's example of crumpling the can and throwing it off into the undergrowth. He could tell he was losing his friend's attention and decided to change the subject.

"Pass us another there, Spence."

Spence reached into the carrier bag and absentmindedly passed a can across. He cracked open his own and took a deep swig then sat back, his arms stretched along the back of the bench.

"Would you look at the state of that?" he said, with something like hunger in his voice.

Tony followed his gaze towards a blonde twenty-something.

"Fucking hell," Tony said, his eyes following the curves of her behind as it disappeared behind a tree.

"Fucking heaven, more like," Spence said.

The girl reappeared a heartbeat later, glorious in her

shorts and vest, sweat beading at the nape of her neck. Both men sat wordlessly until she had disappeared from sight. A leaf floated down from the branches above them and landed on Tony's nose.

"Pft," he said, spitting air at the leaf. "Pft," he repeated as two college girls walked by on their way to class, bags swinging against their waists. "Pft," Tony said a third time. "That's what we need, Spence, some girls like that to pass the day with. We could have a good time with some girls like that, and these beers, out here in the sun... or in doors in the dark," he sniggered.

Spence was still distracted, staring after the girls as they disappeared into an underpass. "I should have gone to college."

Tony laughed. "Right mate, today we'll get some girls. I guarantee it."

Spence raised his eyebrows as he took another can from the carrier bag.

Tony hurriedly finished his drink off.

"Hey, what happened to that girl at the gym in the end? The one you told me about? The little brunette?"

"Pah," Spence said, spitting out a little of the beer without meaning to. "Turns out she's frigid. I was working on my lats the other day..." – he had been, Tony could tell – "and she came over asking if I was alright and did I need anything? So of course I says, 'I'm all good here, darling' and she walks away. So anyway, when I'd finished she was just clearing up all the medicine balls and having a bit of a sweep, you know, and I caught her and said 'So when are we gonna make it happen?' Well, she kidded on like she didn't know what I was talking about, so I broke it down for her and told her we were getting a drink this week. Well, suddenly she's got a boyfriend. Anyway we got into a bit of an argument but the long and short of it is I had to leave and she's a frigid bitch."

"Fucking cow," Tony repeated as a group of kids thundered past after a football.

They sat quietly for a moment and Tony thought of his

6

own gym. The redhead who always happened to be on the cross-trainer in front of him while he was on the rowing machine. What an arse. Jesus Christ. The things he would do to her. He hadn't spoken to her yet, but when he did... Jesus... just wait and see. He became lost for a moment in his memories from the rowing machine. He could feel something begin to stir. It wouldn't have been a good look in his short shorts, there in the park, so he decided to change the subject.

In the end Spence saved him the trouble. "Look at that soft prick," he said, gesturing across the park to where a skinny guy in green shorts and an orange t-shirt had stooped to pick something up from the ground. A small dog yapped beside him.

Tony didn't know what sort of dog it was. They were all the same to him. "Ha-ha, what an idiot, picking up shit," he laughed. "You're in the park, mate. Outdoors! Just leave it," he pretended to call across to the guy. "Jeeze," he said, wiping his eyes.

"Wait a fucking minute, though," Spence said. He grabbed hold of Tony's shoulder and pulled him close, whispering with a note of disbelief in his voice. "Look at that daft prick!"

Tony pulled his shoulder free and looked back across to the guy with the dog. He was standing again, but beside him knelt an incredible blonde, hair spilling over her shoulders as she held the dog's face in both hands. It looked to Tony as though she was trying to unscrew its head by shaking it from side to side.

"Jesus," Spence said.

From where they sat Tony and Spence were too far away to make out what the woman was saying, but from time to time she looked up from the dog to the man and laughed at the things coming out of his mouth.

"The jammy prick," Spence said.

They continued their voyeurism until the woman stood up, passed something to the man and left, looking back over her shoulder for a final smile.

"Jesus," Spence repeated, "That's what we need, some dogs. The birds love dogs," he said, laughing at his animal joke.

Tony's mind was elsewhere. The woman kneeling down had brought up a strange memory, one that he couldn't quite connect. It had happened fifteen years ago, at his mum's funeral. He barely remembered the day. There were a lot of people in black. And it had rained. A lot. All day rain fell and a man had told him off for having mud on his shoes. It wasn't his dad, though. He was off somewhere. He remembered how someone had said he was 'Doing porridge' and his eight-year-old mind hadn't understood. Another thing his eight-year-old mind hadn't understood was the feeling that suddenly came over him when his aunt knelt beside him and took his hand in hers, telling him how sorry she was and how he'd have to be a big boy now. It hadn't been her words that stuck in his mind, but rather the way her dress slipped aside and revealed the smooth curves beneath. Tight curls of red hair rested on her shoulders and he had noticed –or he had imagined since – a stray strand of red hair gently brushed across the firm breasts.

He hadn't known what to do with this image aged eight. He didn't know what the feeling that came over him had been and so he stored it away to bring out at another time and ponder over. He thought about it often and a few years later he understood what it meant and stored it away for future use. Even now he thought about it from time to time.

"Another one!" Spence yelped.

The noise brought Tony back to the present. Another man, this one at least in his forties, made his way through the park, a big furry dog running ahead on a lead. Every now and then middle-aged women out for their power-walk would stop and point to the dog and Tony could almost feel their excitement. The man passed close by their bench just as the college girls returned. They too stopped and cooed at the dog.

Spence stared at the girls' behinds and when they had gone and the man and his dog had disappeared into another part of the park, he stood up and dusted down his trousers.

"Right that's me, mate. I'm off."

"But," Tony said and he glanced at his watch, "it's not even three."

"I'm not sitting here to have my face rubbed in it by all these pricks with dogs," Spence said. "I'll see you soon."

"OK," Tony said as he watched Spence move off down the path.

Tony still had another beer left and he sat back comfortably in the sun and drank it slowly. As he thought about the afternoon's events an idea slowly came over him. At first he wasn't sure if it was his own idea or one he'd seen on television, or somewhere. He didn't have many of his own ideas and he turned this one around in his head for a long time, to make sure it was his, and to pick out any holes in it. After a while Tony was sure and he threw the empty beer can into a bush and went home to think about his aunt.

***

The next day Tony woke early and hurried his breakfast down, his spoon shaking with excitement. He stopped every now and then between mouthfuls to laugh to himself. When he'd finished eating he went back to his bedroom and made his bed, spraying some cologne on the sheets. An old trick. Afterwards he got dressed in front of the mirror. His gym membership was paying off and he tensed and turned and posed until he was ready to put his clothes on. A while later he left the house and made his way to the string of pet shops by the river.

A bell sounded as Tony opened the door of the first shop and stepped into a noise of high pitched chirps and barks and screeches. A smell of wet sawdust met him as he made his way down the rows of white cages filled with cats and rabbits. Tony had never had any pets, except some goldfish that had died quite suddenly, the same day as his mother. He looked in the cages at the kittens, piled up on top of one another, pulling on each other's ears with their teeth. Tony could not see the attraction. He felt nothing for the rabbits, either. He'd eaten rabbit a few times but as he looked at the furry balls hopping about in their cages he couldn't even manage to feel hungry. Instead, he imagined he could taste fur and he began to spit the imaginary fur from his mouth, wiping his tongue on his front teeth."

"Can I help you?" A voice asked from behind him.

Tony turned to find a short woman in a long white coat. The uniform looked more like that of a scientist and with all the animals in their sterile white cages, Tony was reminded of an animal testing lab and laughed quietly to himself.

The woman was waiting and Tony realised he hadn't answered her. "Oh," he said, "erm, I'm after a dog."

"Right…" the woman said. She half turned and gestured to the back wall of the shop. "Well this is where we keep all the dogs, is there a particular breed you wanted?"

"Not particularly," Tony said, following her to the back where he was surrounded by cages and cages of little yappy dogs, all of which seemed to come alive as Tony and the shop assistant came near. Tony winced at the noise.

"There wasn't anything in particular you were after?" the assistant asked and Tony noticed for the first time that she was quite attractive. She had short, curly black hair that tucked itself under her jaw. Beneath her white coat a red t-shirt seemed to hide moderately-sized breasts. She'd be alright without her glasses, Tony decided.

"There wasn't really anything in particular, no," Tony said. "I was just looking for some companionship" (and he smiled inside his head at the line).

"Aww, bless you," the woman said, her eyes crinkling at the corners.

"What can you tell me about this one?" Tony said, pointing to a small, ugly little dog.

The dog wasn't doing anything but lying on its stomach, its head resting on its front paws and Tony felt a sudden affinity with it. "He's an ugly little bastard, isn't he?"

The shop assistant winced. "Not everyone thinks so.

This one is a pug. They're very highly sought-after, actually."

Tony noticed the price written on the side of the cage in black felt-tip. "Jesus Christ," he said. "People pay that, do they? For a dog?"

The woman nodded. "They do."

"Not me," Tony said, then feeling things were going well with the woman, he added, "I'm Tony, by the way."

"Meredith," the woman said, leaving Tony's hand where it hung.

"Well, Meredith, what else can you show me?" Tony asked, with what he thought was a hint of cheekiness in his voice.

He was shown all the dogs they had on offer, Meredith telling him a little bit about each breed until Tony became so bored he thought he might abandon the plan all together. Finally he picked a little mongrel dog, the cheapest in the shop. At the checkout Meredith tried to sell him some extras.

"How about a dog bed? Dog food?"

"Just the dog," Tony said.

"But you'll need them," Meredith said

"Just the dog," Tony repeated as he handed her the money. "And a lead," he added quickly. "Keep the little bastard safe."

When the transaction was over Tony was about to suggest Meredith meet him after work, but before he could speak she said, "Goodbye" and walked off into the storeroom.

"Suit yourself, love," Tony thought and he walked out into the sunshine, his new pet running beside him on its lead.

It didn't take Tony long to get to the park and almost immediately his plan began to work. The girl he'd seen running the previous day was jogging through the park again. She stopped when she saw him and came and knelt down beside the dog.

"Oh my god!" she said, her breasts heaving with the

effort of her exercise.

"What's he called?" she asked, looking up at Tony who stood dumbfounded, surprised his plan was working.

"Erm…" he said. He hadn't thought of a name. It hadn't even occurred to him that pets had names. "Spence," he said. It was the first thing that came to mind.

"Oh hello, Spence!" the girl said, tickling the dog's stomach as it jumped up and licked the sweat from her chest, sending the girl into a laughing fit.

Lucky bastard, Tony thought.

"What sort of dog is he?" the girl asked, her green eyes meeting Tony's.

"He's a mongrel… like me."

"Oh," the girl said, and she laughed again. She patted Spence the dog on the head and stood up and began jogging on the spot.

"Well nice to meet you Spence and…"

It took Tony a second to realise before he blurted out, "Tony. My name's Tony. Nice to meet you."

They shook hands and the girl began to run away.

"See you around, Spence!" she shouted over her shoulder.

Afterwards Tony had to sit down for a minute or two to assess the success of his plan. Thus far, it was working. But still, he hadn't sealed any deals. That was stage two. And there was no time like the present to see it through.

Spence the dog jumped up against his leg and Tony shook him off violently. The dog didn't seem to mind and jumped up again. Tony reached down and unclipped the dog's lead. Tony made his way to the path beside the road. Spence followed obediently and Tony was surprised that he didn't run off.

Tony and the dog walked up and down the road beside the park a few times. It wasn't a busy road and for his plan to work he'd have to time two events perfectly. After four times up and down the road, Tony thought he had his opportunity. Making her way towards him down the path was a tall redhead, strolling confidently along, heels clicking and handbag glinting in the sunlight. She was perfect and, even better, she hadn't noticed Tony, yet. Spence the dog bounded along happily beside his master.

The redhead came closer. Just then, with perfect timing, a car came cruising down the road. It wasn't going too fast, but it would be fast enough. The driver was looking at something on the other side of the road. Tony had a quick look around, and deciding the coast was clear, he stepped over Spence the dog, so that the dog was closest to the road, and kicked him sharply in the stomach.

"Fuck off, Spence," he said through gritted teeth.

The force of his kick had lifted the dog up like a football. Spence hung in the air for a second, yelping in confusion, before the bonnet of the car connected with a bang and sent him skidding down the road.

The driver screeched to a halt and Tony ran to the broken and quivering body of the dog. He knelt beside Spence as the dog tried to lift its head. Tony knew the part he had to play now.

"Oh God! Oh God, I'm sorry, I didn't see him!" the driver cried as he paced back and forth besides the dog, running his hands through his hair, the car door left open behind them.

"Well," Tony began, trying to force tears to his eyes.

He was interrupted by a voice from behind. "You idiot! You absolute idiot!"

The redhead was beside him, jabbing a filed fingernail into the driver's chest.

"It was an accident, lady! An accident!"

"Tell that to the police!" the woman said.

Tony remained kneeling beside the dog while this went on behind him. The dog's stomach hung out in a purple and black puddle. There wasn't as much blood as Tony expected. Spence's whining slowed and his breathing became shallower.

"You poor man!"

Tony felt the woman's hand on his shoulder. She knelt beside him, her red hair tumbling over her breasts, and suddenly Tony's tears were real and the woman was pulling him into her chest and patting his head.

"There there. There there."

After a minute Spence's breathing stopped and he lay there dead.

"Oh God!" the woman said. She helped Tony to his feet. "If you need someone to be a witness, for the police…" she began.

"It. Was. An. Accident!" the driver yelled, tearing at his hair now.

"It's OK," Tony said. "I think I just want to go home now."

"Of course, of course," the redhead said, taking his hand in hers. "We'll go get a coffee, let *him* collect your poor dog," she said jabbing a vicious finger in the direction of the driver.

The driver had found a black plastic bag and had brought the remains of Spence the dog to the café where the woman bought Tony drink after drink. After a fierce reprimand from the woman and an exchange of phone numbers for compensation, the driver left, sheepishly scratching his head.

Back at Tony's house they held a funeral. The woman weeping gently into Tony's arm. By now Tony's authentic tears had stopped and he was able to coax the woman towards the obvious conclusion as they threw soil over the shoebox that held Spence the dog.

In the morning Tony woke to the sight of the woman slipping back into her dress. He watched her a second before she noticed he was awake. When she did she came and sat beside him and laid a hand on his head as though he had a fever.

"You poor thing. Are you all right?"

"I think so," Tony said, swallowing his grin solemnly.

"I have to go to work today," the woman said, fishing around in her bag for something. "But here's my card. Call me."

She smiled and then she was gone.

14

Tony rolled over and went back to sleep.

***

After the third day Meredith at the pet shop was becoming suspicious. She'd become cold towards Tony and the last time he came in she went straight into the stockroom and let a teenage boy serve him instead. By now Tony had bought the three cheapest dogs in the shop and the cost was starting to pile up. It was then he got the idea to go to the pound to collect his dogs. He found this much more agreeable, as the dogs there were free. They were mainly mangy specimens that no one would miss. This didn't bother Tony, although each day he chose the proudest looking dog he could, then walked his new pet smugly out of the building, the chorus of the hundreds of other dogs yet to be chosen following them out.

Tony had brought a different woman back every day since he'd first kicked Spence into the road. By now he was on the seventh Spence and each morning after the girl had left, he had to pull up and throw away the crosses they'd made to mark the graves in his garden. By the seventh day it was getting hard for Tony to remember where he'd buried each dog and he dreaded digging up a decomposing leg or ear, with a girl sobbing beside him.

He'd also had to start rotating which parks he used each day, to avoid any of the regulars spotting him and his trick. Nevertheless, the phone numbers piled up in Tony's bedside drawer. There had been a few girls who had even stopped and given him their number when he'd been walking through the park with whichever Spence he had at the time. Tony decided not to bother with these girls. Why spend money and energy taking them to a film, drink or meal when he could get what he wanted with an unwitting motorist and a flick of his foot?

The real Spence had called a few times through the week and each time Tony had brushed him off. He was busy, he said. There wasn't a chance he would share his tricks with Spence. He'd just walk up one day, one of his girls on his arm, and Spence wouldn't know what to say.

"Spence," Tony would say, with a little nod of his head. And before Spence could say anything he'd be on his way again.

On the eighth day, Tony got out of bed around midday. A condom was stuck to his leg, left over from the night before and he peeled it off and flung it across the room. He took his usual route to the pound. The staff there knew him by now and nodded as he came in. They assumed he was running some sort of dog rescue, or giving them away as presents.

Tony nodded at the old man who greeted him from behind the counter. It was a shame there weren't any young girls here, he thought, "I could have my pick." He did have his pick of the dogs, though, and that day he went for a particularly glossy Jack Russell. Once it was free of its cage, Tony grabbed the dog roughly and attached the lead. They walked out into the summer sunshine, Tony dragging the dog behind him. It was going to be a beautiful day.

They set off down the street and hadn't gone far before Tony noticed Meredith from the pet shop making her way towards him.

"Stuck up bitch," Tony said to himself and turned in the opposite direction, yanking the dog around.

He hadn't taken more than four steps in that direction before he noticed a mess of red hair coming towards him down the street. It was the woman from the first night. Tony hadn't called any of his women yet and panic immediately overcame him. What would he say to her? How would he explain the new dog so soon after the heartbreak of losing his previous companion? He couldn't play the same trick twice on the same girl, could he? Tony turned back up the street but there was Meredith again and their eyes met in an awkward instant. There was only one direction he could go, so Tony plunged out into the road, dragging the dog behind him.

The driver didn't see him. Thoughts of hitting and

killing a dog earlier in the week haunted him and kept him awake at nights and now, as a result of this stress, he was nervous behind the wheel, frantically glancing about as he drove. Looking everywhere but the road.

The car struck Tony just above the knees and sent him hurtling through the air to land some ten feet away, twisted and broken, in the middle of the road. Luckily, the impact of the car had made Tony release his grip on the dog's lead and the Jack Russell stood by the side of the road for a moment, licked his lips and then wandered happily off down the street.

Passers-by rushed to the crumpled body. The redhead was the first to the scene and upon recognising Tony she burst into tears and cradled his head in her lap as blood bubbled slowly out of his mouth.

"Oh God!" she cried. "Hold on. Just hold on. You'll be all right, you precious man."

But Tony had never been good at taking instructions and his eyelids were becoming heavy so he decided to let them close.

***

Spence was just coming back from the gym, admiring his shining muscles in shop windows as he made his way down the road. Suddenly there was a bang followed by a screech of brakes and the screech of screams. Spence dropped his gym bag and ran towards the noise. A beautiful redhead knelt in the road, tears washing lines through her foundation, mascara dripping off the end of her nose. Even like that she looked good. There was a crowd of people gathered on the periphery and in the centre the woman cradled someone's head in her lap. Spence immediately made his way to her.

"It's OK. It's OK," he said, putting his arm around her shoulder. Fucking Tony, what a way to go...

The woman glanced up at him, then back to the body in her arms. Spence pulled her towards him and cradled her head on his shoulder.

"It's OK," he said again. "It's OK."

The woman's eyes met his and her hold on the head in her lap loosened.

"It's OK," she repeated, wiping the tears from her eyes.

A Week Abroad

He raised the cup to his lips and took a sip of the coffee. He held the cup there a moment and looked at her over the rim, like a spy glancing over the top of a newspaper. She was sitting a few tables along, half hidden in the shade of the parasol. Where the sun hit her, it lit her up like dynamite.

He lowered the cup. That's right, she was dynamite.

He glanced over again, trying only to move his eyes, not his head. No one wants to look like they're staring. She was beautiful. Anyone could see what all the fuss was about; the way her bare shoulder caught the sun, her skin like powdered snow on a mountain top. Her red dress tight around her breasts. Her cream silk scarf tied firmly around her neck, like a bow on a gift. Hair like black lace. A mouth to die for. He could just about make out red lipstick on the tip of the cigarette she held nonchalantly in her left hand, the smoke drifting with no rush, penetrated by the bright sun's rays, forming a mist around her; an aura of mystery, or danger.

He saw all of this from the corner of his eyes. And as always, he saw more than this. The white tulip brooch she wore on her dress. The black high heels, now hidden under her table. No more than four inches. She was roughly five feet six inches herself, so two inches short of six foot with the heels.

He lifted the cup from the shiny ring of coffee in his saucer and took another sip. Coffee was about to drip from the bottom of the cup so he took a napkin and wiped it and then wiped the saucer. Three times. Clockwise motion.

A dog barked in the square and a flock of pigeons flew up from the fountain, the flap of their wings mingling with the trickle of the clear water. The water had an almost-green tint to it. Not a polluted green; a nice green, like the colour of a jade statute. He liked it. Colours were important to him. He had always enjoyed all sorts of details that most people did not notice.

The dog left the square, disappearing down the third alleyway to the west. He was pleased; animals annoyed him. Never work with children or animals. The only distraction now was the little yappy dog the two women next to him had brought along. Breeds weren't his strong point, but it looked like a Chihuahua, and the two women yapped along with it. They had arrived with it in one of their designer handbags. He hated to imagine the mess the dog had left in there. He thought about this now, and wiped his hands on his trousers under the table.

She had loved it when the women had sat down beside her, the Chihuahua poking its head out of the bag, yelping and scrambling to escape. She'd moved her chair closer and commenced stroking the foul little animal while she asked the women its name, breed and price.

The two older women droned on for minutes in response, leaning forwards and obstructing his view. They were old money but tasteless. She knew what was in good taste. He imagined she was only being polite about the dog. The worst thing was that the women let it wander about freely. There was no control, no discipline. He felt it now, sniffing against his shoes. His freshly polished Oxfords. He imagined the dog's wet nose dripping onto his foot and gave it a quick jab in the ribs with his toe. The dog yelped and went scurrying back to the women at the next table. They looked shocked and stared over at him with heavy, frowning brows. He smiled across at them and held their gaze until they looked away and began muttering to the dog, "Ah, ma Cherie!"

He turned away and took another sip of his coffee. It was strong. Better than anything he'd tasted in England. He finished the cup but kept it held to his lips so he could watch her over the rim. A waiter came out of the café and went over to her table. He could not hear what was being said but knew they were both speaking French. She smiled at the waiter as he poured her another espresso and stretched her legs out under the table. The yappy dog ran over and licked her heels but she didn't seem to notice. He would have liked to kill the dog.

He put his cup down and looked out over the square. It was empty apart from a few couples walking in the sun. He could hear the dog yapping again and he ground his teeth. He had to remind himself about this. Breathe in. One, two. He felt his pulse slow down and ran a hand through his blond hair, making sure it was still slicked back. He could feel a slight sweat on his brow. For God's sake, this was no good, if she saw him looking nervous... He took his handkerchief from his breast pocket and dabbed the corners of his forehead before returning the handkerchief to the same pocket he'd taken it from. Then he straightened his narrow tie.

A second waiter came out of the café, carrying a tray with cakes and coffee for the two women. It was the blond waiter. He worked Mondays, Tuesdays, Wednesdays and Saturdays, and today was a Wednesday. The other waiter worked every day and the skinny one was not here. That particular waiter only worked Friday to Monday. Research had told him that she knew them all. He knew that she had been a regular here each day for the past two weeks, normally between twelve and two. Before those two weeks she had been in the town a month. He knew all of this but it was the first time he'd been to the café and he had only been in the town a week.

The older women cooed as the waiter placed their cakes on the table. One of them touched the waiter's arm and the other laughed at something unheard. The waiter smiled at them.

It was disgusting and, watching from his own table, he had to grip his knee under the table to control himself. The waiter finished at the table and turned to go back inside.

He called out to him as he passed. "Monsieur, café s'il

21

vous plait."

The waiter nodded. "Oui" then went back into the cafe.

He'd had to turn in his seat to call to the waiter, and now something dug into his ribs. He could not reach inside his jacket to move it, so he sat back in the chair and ignored the discomfort.

Her cigarette smoke drifted across to him and he inhaled it deeply without trying to look like he was doing so. It tasted sweet. The coffee was sweet as well. Everything was too sweet. The women next to him, each with a sweet tooth. He checked his watch. It was almost two; she would be leaving soon, going back to her hotel. He glanced over at her. She seemed to be in no rush. She leant back leisurely in her chair and smoked her cigarette, letting the smoke escape through red lips. The lips were like a wound and he thought of his own wound, the scar across his left cheek. It was not yet fully healed and always turned bright red in the sun. He wondered if she had noticed it. If she had noticed him. It would be better if not.

"Monsieur, votre café." It was the waiter. He placed the new cup on the table and took up the old one.

"Merci."

The waiter smiled, his blond hair shining in the sun, "Ah, you are English, non?"

He said nothing.

"I have seen you admiring the woman over there." He rolled his eyes to indicate the direction and then winked. "Yes, she is very beautiful, she comes here every day," the waiter continued. "They say she is famous. Perhaps she will give you an autograph; she is English too, non?"

He took a sip of the coffee then put down the cup. He gave the waiter his smile. The same one he had given the women.

"Is she? I can't say I know who she is. I'm not sure she is famous at all, I hadn't really noticed her until just now."

He saw the look of confusion creep over the waiter's face and added, "But yes, she is rather beautiful, I suppose."

The waiter smiled and nodded. "Oui, monsieur, très

belle!"

He smiled back and after a few seconds the waiter nodded, said "Monsieur," and went back inside.

She stood up now and stubbed out her cigarette on her saucer. He checked his watch. It was 2pm. exactly. The women called over to her and she came over and kissed them goodbye, not quite touching their cheeks. Air kisses. Then she tucked her slender legs under her, her dress riding slightly up her thighs as she bent down to lift the dog up and kiss it goodbye.

He could have almost been sick. He drank the rest of his coffee in one, ignoring the heat, and watched her as she walked past him and across the square. She hadn't looked at him. He took out his wallet and placed a twenty euro note under his saucer, then took out his sunglasses from his inside jacket pocket. He put them on and brushed his hair back then counted to ten before rising and following her across the square.

She was the other side of the fountain now and about to turn down the second alley. He was in no rush to catch her. The idea was to keep some distance. Besides, he could easily hear the rhythmic click of her heels on the cobbled street. He matched her pace and followed her, watching the curves of her behind as she walked. She turned a corner. It did not matter if she got away; he knew which was her hotel.

He was certain it was her. He had watched her for a week without her realising. The first time he saw her he'd checked her against the photograph he carried in his wallet and was sure. He should have burnt the picture after that but he couldn't bring himself to do it; he was lonely at nights in this town where he knew no one. He remembered when the fat man had given him the picture. He had sat in the office somewhere in Charing Cross. It was night outside but the fat man had called him in. 'Urgent business'. The office was dark and the lights were dim. The deep green of the leather made the chair seem uncomfortable. It was all too formal.

The fat man had sat back behind his desk and offered

him a whisky. He didn't drink. A haze of cigar smoke filled the room and the taste stung his throat. It'd been a bitter taste, not like the sweetness of her cigarette. The fat man had forgotten about it once he started talking and the stub lay smouldering in a gold ash tray.

The fat man had leant forward over the desk, stroking his yellow and black tie. He'd been biting his nails. The fat of his cheeks wobbled as he spoke and continued moving a split second after his jaw had stopped. The fat man had explained everything and then raised his eyebrows as if inviting questions but he had none. It was simple enough. The fat man had reached into a drawer in his desk and took out a small photograph which he slid across the desk.

"Recognise her?"

"No," he answered.

"You're perfect for this," the fat man laughed.

He'd looked at the picture for a second before slipping it into his inside pocket. She was beautiful; there was no doubt about it, but money was more beautiful to him.

The fat man spoke again, "You have ten days. This needs to be done."

He nodded and rose to leave.

"Ten days," the fat man repeated.

He smiled at him, left the office as silently as a wisp of smoke, and stepped out into the wet London night.

He continued after her through the French town, occasionally losing sight of her, but always hearing the click-click-click of her heels. They walked through winding alleyways but neither of them was lost. He had rehearsed this walk many times over the past week. They came to her hotel, a five-star palace with golden lions outside and a red carpet lining the steps up to the entrance. She walked slowly up the steps with practiced grace and the doorman bowed as he opened the door for her. She smiled and touched him lightly on the shoulder. He saw this and tried not to clench his fist. He took off his sunglasses and put them in his left jacket pocket as he walked up the steps.

The doorman was trying to stop himself smiling as he

nodded, 'Monsieur'.

He slipped a fifty euro note into the doorman's pocket as he passed. The doorman thanked him with a straight face.

She wasn't too far ahead of him now, he could see her at the desk as the Concierge handed her the room key. She held it in such a way that he could only make out one of the numbers on the tag. It didn't matter; he knew exactly which room she was staying in. There was no need to pretend to be occupied while he watched the numbers change above the elevator. He made sure he was out of her field of vision as the elevator arrived and she stepped in and turned to face outwards. Then the golden doors closed and the first few numbers lit up one by one as she headed to her floor.

He took the stairs. Slowly. Let her get settled in her room. Let her get halfway through pouring a drink or drawing a bath. It wouldn't do to be seen hurrying up the stairs, either. Not in a place like this and not in any place he'd worked. It dug into his ribs again as he walked but it was just something you had to deal with. Six floors. Four more to go. He was making good time. Quick, but not too quick. He wasn't sweating; he was too fit for that.

After the ground floor the stairs had been sectioned off from the corridor of each floor and a door led out at the top of each flight. He reached the sixth floor. 607. He stood a moment at the door and listened. He could hear no one. It was silent above and below him. He took off his shoes and placed them neatly beside the door. He slid the door open gently and quietly, and stepped out into the sixth floor corridor.

He paused to check his appearance in a wall-length mirror and straightened his tie. His hair was all right for now. He was just a businessman heading to his room.

607 was around a bend in the corridor and he padded quietly across the carpet in his socks and stopped at the corner. He still could not hear anything but there would be no harm in waiting a few more minutes. The last thing he wanted was a maid to come bustling out of a room and surprise everyone. Or an American family on their holidays.

When they got scared they were worse than an alarm. But no one was around. He was certain. It was the middle of the day and most people would be out visiting the town. He took a last look around the corner and leant back against the wall.

He always kept a pair of leather gloves in his trouser pockets and he took them out now. They were the only thing he had in there, other than a wallet which contained only one hundred euros cash and the photograph. He slipped the gloves on and stretched his fingers out in them to make sure they slid fully into place. Still no sound. It was time to earn his money. He reached his right hand into the left side of his jacket and brought his Beretta pistol out of its holster.

His mind was clear as an empty glass vase. He pulled back the slide and checked the round in the chamber. Still no noise in the corridor. He kept a silencer in his holster which he took out and screwed slowly onto the pistol, using his thumb and forefinger. Three turns. Clockwise motion. He held the pistol in his left hand and undid his buttons so that his jacket swung open. He checked the safety was still on and tucked the pistol into his waistband.

He glanced back down the corridor and then around the corner but did not see anyone. It was time. He walked around the corner and quickly moved over to the light switch. He flicked it off and the lights went out, leaving the corridor in darkness except for the emergency signs and the elevator lights. He padded slowly up to her door, his back to the wall. 607. He ran a gloved hand through his hair and put his ear to the door. There was no light coming from under the door. He assumed she must be in the bathroom.

He stood for a full minute with his ear against the door and his mouth open to reduce cavity noise, enabling him to hear what was going on in the room, rather than his own breathing. There was no one moving inside. He could get in, sneak up on her quietly and catch her unawares. It was a shame really – all that beauty going to waste. They told him she was talented, too. Maybe if she hadn't expanded her talents into the fat man's area of expertise she would have lived to become an icon. He brushed his hair back. Never mind.

He took the pistol out and turned off the safety. Then he knelt and laid the pistol next to him, at a right angle to the door, within arm's reach. Slowly, he reached into his side jacket pocket and took out a thin piece of metal wire which he inserted into the lock with the steady hand of a surgeon. He made subtle movements with the wire, slightly to the left, a little bit upwards. He worked for thirty seconds until he heard a soft click, telling him the lock was open. Now he had to act quickly. He placed the wire back in his pocket and picked up the pistol, making certain the safety catch was off. Still no sound from inside.

His gloved left hand turned the door knob slowly as he pushed the door open with his right shoulder. He stepped into the room and raised the hand holding the pistol, gently kicking the door shut with his heel as he did so. The room was dark and he quickly scanned each corner from the doorway. She wasn't there. The sound of running water came from the bathroom and light shone into the room from the doorway to the left. He took a step towards it, treading slowly in his socks. His focus was on the door, a hundred different scenarios playing through his mind as he prepared to burst through into the bathroom.

He took another step towards the door and the sound of running water, when suddenly there was a new noise, a sort of 'phish' sound that seemed to come from inside the room. It was followed immediately by another. He wondered where it had come from. It was a sound he knew well but he was confused as to where it had come from without him making it. She was in the bathroom, surely. He turned on his heel to scan the room again but felt unsteady as his knee twisted under him. His pistol dropped to the floor with a soft thud as it landed in the deep carpet. He took a step towards the wardrobe, feeling weaker now. Then, his knees buckled and he knelt on the carpet. The carpet was deep and white but there were flecks of red – little drops – as though someone had flicked a brush dripped in red paint across the room.

A soft cough escaped his mouth and as he held up a gloved hand he was surprised to see the same red shining on the black leather. He wasn't able to kneel anymore and fell backwards to lie on the carpet, his long legs tucked under him. He could smell her now, a soft perfume that he'd never smelled before. It was strange he hadn't smelled it; he had been so well prepared. Everything was fully researched. It was all in the details, all in the preparation. He hadn't let himself become distracted. The smell grew stronger, undercut with the sweet undertones of cigarettes.

He pushed himself up on one elbow but a third 'phish' knocked him back. The carpet was wet. Funny. What kind of hotel was this? His breathing was heavy now. It felt like something was bubbling in his chest. He tried to see what the problem was but could only move his head to the side.

A pair of black heels stepped from behind a dressing screen and as he moved his eyes, he saw they led up to a pair of slender legs. They approached slowly over the carpet and he could make out the hem of a red dress.

She was standing next to him now. The perfume overwhelmed him. It became a part of him. It was inside him and seemed to bleed out of him. He breathed deeply but couldn't quite catch his breath. A shiny black high heel touched his head and rolled it back so that he was looking straight up. He couldn't see the ceiling; his vision was blocked by the red dress, reaching up almost as far as he could see. Two red cushions seemed to be floating in the darkness where the dress ended. They seemed to smile down at him and he smiled back weakly. The first genuine smile that he could remember.

Then, something black blocked his vision, something cylindrical and cold-looking. He tried to stretch his neck to see around it, to see her again, but he couldn't move. He let out a last, rasping breath and looked into the barrel of her gun. A millisecond later a final 'phish' echoed softly around the room while his blood seeped into the carpet like the slow spread of spilt red wine.

Four Night Stand

It was around 8pm when the message came through. It was Laura Thompson. She'd been drinking all day with her friends and did I want to come over? Did I want to go over? I wasn't really in the mood. I'd met her in town a few weeks back and we'd shared a handful of drunken encounters since. I didn't know if I could face her sober; we'd never actually had a proper conversation.

To hell with it, I decided. I'd been reading Chinaski and knew what he would have done. I told her I'd be round in a while, I just had to get rid of my friend. My friend was a bottle of red I had, but she didn't need to know that. I got the bottle, took a hit. This was shaping up to be quite an evening.

The wine was taking hold. I put some music on to get me in the mood. I supposed I had better get dressed. I'd have to do my hair. Did I have any condoms left? This girl was bleeding me dry. I had no money whatsoever and had to keep doing chlamydia tests in bars to get the free condoms they handed out. I'd have to line up some more. Hopefully the results would keep being negative.

Another text came through, telling me to come round at half past ten when her friends had left. Fine with me. It was awkward enough talking to Laura; I didn't want to imagine conversation with her friends.

I got on with the wine and music then had a bit of a wash and sprayed some deodorant. When it came time to go I walked downstairs. My parents were watching TV.

"I'm off out to Jack's."

"At this time?"

"Yeah."

"Don't drink and drive."

I laughed as I walked out the door. I could see the curtain twitching as I reversed down the driveway. Jack's house was to the right, Laura's to the left. I headed right and let the throttle out down the long straight road and then came all the way back round and past my house again.

Laura lived out in the country. I had to cross a bridge and there was a tight turn after it that always caught me off guard. The night I'd met her I'd driven us home. I'd only been a little drunk but there were a few moments when she'd screamed. I liked it. It made me go faster.

I got to her house and looked through the window. She lived with her best friend's family. There was no way I was going to knock for some middle-aged guy to come answer the door. I called her.

"It's me, I'm here, come let me in."

She laughed.

"You pussy. I'll be two minutes."

It was more like two seconds. She opened the door and I walked in.

"Hi. All right?"

"I'm all right. How about you?"

We walked through to the next room. There was a girl sat on the sofa. We were introduced. Laura was wearing white shorts and a t-shirt. Her thighs looked a little flabbier than I remembered. This was the fourth time I'd been round and already she wasn't putting as much effort in. Her friend looked good though. Maybe I'd come out here when I'd finished with Laura. Chinaski would've.

Laura fixed me a Malibu and lemonade. It was either that or Archers. We went off to her room. I said goodnight to her friend and she replied with a knowing smile.

The door closed and Laura sat on her bed and made small talk.

"I have a joke for you. Someone told me it and it made me think of you and your terrible jokes."

"Go on," I said

"What do you call a bull that's asleep? A bulldozer."

I couldn't help but smile.

"Mine were solid gold compared to that."

"Oh yeah, something about fish."

She reached over and turned on the TV. It was *Family Guy*. More comedy. We finished our drinks.

"How many have you had today?"

"Well, we started drinking before lunch."

"Before lunch? Shit. I've only been awake a few hours, and you've spent the whole day drinking."

"You'll be taking advantage of me again," she said, smiling.

Laura wore lots of eye shadow, which I liked. She looked a little bit like a sad clown or a broken-hearted model with her bleach blonde hair. Chinaski would have loved it.

"I'm not gonna feel bad about taking advantage," I said.

"Good, because I only drink to make me want to sleep with you."

I held up the Malibu. "Tell me about it."

She bit my arm. She laughed.

I looked around the room.

"I thought I was lost this morning when I woke up."

"Why?"

"Well, I woke up in my own room and didn't recognise it. I expected to see this mess." She pinched my elbow. We finished our drinks and got down to it.

Afterwards we lay there. She looked at me and laughed for the third time.

"As soon as I took my underwear off you started laughing," I said.

"Fuck off," she said, rolling onto her side.

We lay there awkwardly, not really knowing what to do. I wasn't ready to go again.

"What time is it?" I asked.

"Why? Are you going to have to go back to your mummy?"

"It's suspicious if I stay out on a Monday. I don't want her knowing what I'm doing. Plus, I'm not getting up early

31

when you go to work."

I'd only ever been back at the weekend, when it was easier to pass off a night there as a night on a friend's sofa. A Monday night was not so easy to excuse.

We tried to get down to it again but I wasn't ready and the condom kept coming off. We finally got going but she squirmed too much and the condom came off again. We threw them on the floor. It looked like a pile of let-down balloons. It was embarrassing but I blamed it on the johnnies and she went along with it.

We laid there a while more. She changed the channel on the TV. *Rambo: First Blood Part II* was on. Sly was getting tortured.

"I'll stay until the end of *Rambo*," I joked.

"Ha, maybe you should go home, Sly's making you seem inadequate."

"You're joking. I was the one who trained Sly for this film."

"Oh yeah?" she laughed.

We tried it once more. Sly had escaped and was sitting with his Chinese girlfriend. She was about to get shot and I told her so; but it being a film, I had no effect. We stopped what we were doing and Laura looked pissed off. I made a joke about being too sad to carry on because *Rambo*'s girlfriend was dead. I did my best Sly impression for her. She laughed and we were friends again.

Well almost. There was too much damn pressure on me to get ready for action. All the distractions didn't help. I made a joke about needing her to cheer me up after *Rambo*'s girlfriend bit the dust but she pretended not to get it. Somehow this whole thing had turned into a comedy show and I was dying on stage.

"Look, why don't you go home?"

Was she serious? I kissed her nose. "You'd miss me too much."

She pushed me away. "Ha, you're rubbish."

"This is just like being at school," I said. "Pulling hair and insulting who you fancy."

"Oh, you think I fancy you, do you? You're just a booty call."

"Thank god for that. I thought I'd have to take you out somewhere or something."

"I just don't know what we'd be like sober. We skipped the getting to know each other bit and just started with the…"

"The nocturnal activities? That's the way I like it. You told me you didn't do this sort of thing, and here I am for the fourth time."

"What sort of thing?"

"One night stands."

"This is a four night stand, though, so it's OK because you're the one who's kept crawling back."

"You kept begging me back."

"I'm sure I did."

"What was that text you sent me? 'Please come round I'm in the mood and I've got a shit joke to tell you.' You want me."

"Look are you leaving or are we going to do it again? You're no use to me if not."

We tried and failed again. She wriggled too much for the condoms to stay on. Or maybe my dick was just letting me down. That was the last of them.

"We're out. I'm gonna have to go do another chlamydia test to get some more." It wasn't the best thing I could have said. She looked like I'd just slapped her. I explained the chlamydia test thing and she didn't laugh.

"You're a nerd! Go home to mummy! She's going to be worried!"

She was laughing now. I was pretty sure I could win her round. I was stood next to the bed putting my trousers on. I leant over and gave her a kiss.

"OK, booty call," I said. "Send me a message next time you're drunk."

"I'd have to be. That chlamydia thing's sobered me right up."

"Look that was a joke…"

"I'm not going to text you, you can text me first. You're the booty call but you can call me after you ruined everything with your jokes."

I wasn't sure who was joking at this point.

She put on a robe and walked me to the door.

"Bye, then," she said.

I leant in to kiss her. She seemed to move away a little bit but I got there in the end.

I walked out to my car. Well, it hadn't been a bad night but I was pretty sure it was going to be the last time I'd see her. Comedy had killed my libido. I shouldn't try to do two things at once. I was no Chinaski after all. I drove home and drank the rest of the wine. No harm in trying.

An Appointment With The Family

There was nothing for it. Nothing to be done. William's hair would just not do what he wanted it to. He leaned closer to the mirror, running the comb this way and that. Either his hair stuck up in wild spikes, or it hung limply over his eyes. And why had he shaved? He leaned closer still, his breath misting against the glass. Tiny clusters of belligerent pimples marked his chin. It was a disaster.

This was before he even thought about his tooth.

William opened his mouth slowly, afraid of what he might find. He grimaced at himself in the mirror. The chipped front tooth. It had happened in a drunken brawl. A stupid fight. At first there had been a tiny crack, like that in the paint of an old skirting board. Now the enamel was flaking away like the shell of a hardboiled egg. It was not the look that you wanted when meeting your girlfriend's parents for the first time. It was especially not what you wanted when you considered that her father was a well-respected dentist.

The thought of the meeting filled William with dread. Eva had told him how her father was a difficult man and William was sure that as soon as they were introduced Dr Poots would notice the ugly white splinter in William's mouth and decide there and then that this was not a boy he wanted his daughter to spend time with. Poor personal hygiene was not what fathers looked for when considering whether or not they would let you continue sleeping with their daughter.

William glanced at his watch. It was the eleventh hour, no time for alterations now. He would have to go as he was. He hitched his tie up, grabbed the flowers and wine from the side and hurried out into the street.

The tube train was late, of course, and when it eventually came it was overcrowded with the usual cross section of fed-up commuters. As it approached Clapham the inhabitants of the compartment became whiter and whiter, until William began to suspect that he was unwillingly taking part in some middle class social experiment.

It wasn't quite raining on the common, but all the signs of heavy foreboding were there: an overcast sky, men and women dashing about with their collars turned up, umbrellas struggling against the wind. William persevered through it all, subconsciously probing his chipped tooth with the tip of his tongue.

After a while, he found the street and began searching for the house number. He had hoped it was '230' but life was not a comedy. He passed rows of identical white houses, all set back from the road and enclosed by white brick walls. Palm trees struggled under the October sun and the sports cars standing in the driveways itched for summer.

William found the house. A plaque outside read 'Dr. Benjamin Poots'. William checked the knot of his tie, then smoothed down the paper wrapped around a bunch of flowers. They were white and pristine and William did not know what the proper name for them was.

He took a deep breath, reminding himself that despite his flaws, he was ultimately loveable, and rang the doorbell. A sharp buzz sounded somewhere inside the house. He was about to press the bell again when a hazy shape appeared through the dark green glass set into the door. William relaxed and stepped back, expecting Eva.

When the door opened it took William a moment to realise that he was not face to face with his girlfriend. The woman standing before him was a slightly older version of her, dressed in paint-flecked dungarees which hung loosely about a body that still boasted curves in the proper places. The face was as beautiful as Eva's but with a weathered look of experience that was, if anything, more appealing.

William stepped forward and held out a hand. "Hello,

I'm Wi—"

"William!" the woman cried. "Do come in. I'm Jennifer, Eva's mother."

Jennifer drew him towards her and hugged him to her paint-covered dungarees.

"So nice to meet you!" she said, taking him by the hand and dragging him into the house.

They paused just inside the door and William held out the flowers. "I brought these, for you."

"Oh lilies. I love lilies," she said, holding the flowers beneath her nose and inhaling. "Thank you, William. What a gentleman you are. Eva was right. Where is the little minx? Eva. Eva darling, William is here! I'm sure she'll be down in a minute, William. Now, if you'll excuse me, I must go and take a shower while dinner is finishing off. I've been doing a quick bit of painting," she said, reaching up to tuck a stray strand of hair behind her ear.

William saw her arm was flecked with light blue paint, and that dried red splotches had somehow found their way into her hair.

"I'll be right back, and Eva will be here in a moment. Don't go anywhere!" Jennifer said, moving away along the corridor. 'And thank you for the flowers!' she called over her shoulder.

William glanced about the empty entrance hall. The wallpaper was a dark green, the colour of Christmas wrapping paper and two shelves of dark wood ran the length of the hallway, one on either side. Family pictures featuring a man grinning widely littered the shelves. So that was Benjamin Poots, William thought.

Next to the picture William was looking at stood a taxidermy ferret, baring its teeth fiercely. William imagined he heard a hiss. It was only then that he noticed the rest of the shelf space along the corridor was taken up by taxidermy. Owls, cats, rabbits all arranged in macabre postures, somehow threatening, despite the dust that had gathered amongst the fur.

"They don't bite," a voice said.

"I hope your dad doesn't, either," William said, turning around just in time to catch Eva as she jumped towards him.

They kissed and William felt his worries drop away like old skin.

"Ready to meet everyone?" Eva asked, her eyelashes stroking his cheek.

"I've already met your mother and I can safely say I have no worries about our future," William said, absentmindedly running his hand down Eva's lower back.

"Stop it!" she said, playfully pushing him away. "There'll be time for that later, if you make a good impression."

The front door clattered open. A man and a teenage boy came into the hall, bringing the rain in with them.

"Well, the weather caught us," the man said and William recognised the flash of white teeth.

"Dad, this is William," Eva said, stepping forward to kiss her father's cheek.

Dr Poots looked around as though searching for exactly who his daughter was referring to. His eyes settled on William who smiled weakly as he extended a hand.

"Pleased to meet you, sir."

"No need for 'sir', call me Ben. Good to meet you too, Bill," he said, either missing or ignoring the hand. He shrugged off his wet coat and turned to hang it up.

"It's Will or William, Dad," Eva said, flashing an apologetic smile at William.

He was about to respond with an 'it's-OK-he-seems-nice' smile when Eva spoke again. "This is my brother, Ed. Remember I told you he's a rugby superstar?"

"Yes, I remember," William said. "Good to meet you, Ed," he said, holding out a hand to the younger boy.

"All right, mate?" Ed said, briefly gripping the hand before pushing past and disappearing down the corridor, his wet shorts dripping on the tiled floor.

"Is dinner ready?" Dr Poots asked, his coat folded up and forgotten on a chair by the door.

"Almost. Mum's having a shower," Eva said.

"I brought this for you, sir… Ben. Thank you for having me," William said, offering the bottle of wine.

"Don't thank me yet, Will, you haven't tried Jennifer's cooking." He took the bottle and studied the label.

"Ah, red wine. Stains the teeth," he said, running his tongue over his pristine incisors.

William made shapes with his mouth for a moment, unsure what to say.

Eva rescued him. "Come on, let's go set the table."

***

They gathered around the table. Ed still in his soiled rugby gear, Dr Poots in his shirt sleeves, glancing at his watch. Each time he twisted his arm to check the time, he inadvertently elbowed William in the ribs. William glanced across to Eva, hoping she had seen, but she simply smiled back at him, presumably happy he was yet to insult her father or spill wine over the table.

After Dr Poots had dug him in the ribs for the fourth time, Mrs Poots entered, radiating cleanliness in a worn red jumper, a fleck of paint on her left cheek all that remained of the speckled woman who'd met William at the door.

"Sorry, everybody. Dinner is served!" she said, as she began pulling dishes from the oven.

They began the meal. Penne pasta in a tomato and basil sauce. Satisfied everyone had enough on their plates, Jennifer uncorked William's bottle of wine and leant over the table to fill the glasses. When she came to her husband, he held his hand over the glass and took up the water jug instead. William tried not to notice and focused his attention on the dilemma of eating pasta without turning his shirt red.

"So, William, you're a writer?" Jennifer asked.

He swallowed and nodded enthusiastically. "Yes. I've written a novel, and I've just started writing for a magazine."

"Which magazine?" Dr Poots asked, breaking his silence for the first time since they had started eating.

William hesitated, thinking of the best way to explain the magazine. He was unable to think of a way to phrase it that would reassure Dr Poots that he had the best intentions towards his daughter. Then, a fraction of a second before he was about to speak, Eva told her father the name of the publication.

"A 'lad's mag'," Dr Poots said. It was not a question.

"Not exactly…" William began.

"Yes," Eva answered, happy at the recognition.

"Do you know it, Ed?" Dr Poots asked.

"Mmhhm," Ed answered, his eyes on his plate where he was pushing about a last bit of chicken with his fork.

William must have gone back to nervously probing his tooth because at that moment Dr Poots turned to him, fixed his eyes on William's and asked, "What's the matter?"

William sat back in his chair suddenly. "Nothing's the matter," he tried to say without opening his mouth.

"What, speak up?"

"Dad…" Eva began.

It's nothing, sir. Ben," William said, noticing the cloud slip across Dr Poot's face

"Aha, your tooth!" Dr Poots declared triumphantly. "Let's have a look," he said, leaning across the table towards William.

"Dear, I don't think William wants a dental examination during dinner," Jennifer began.

"It doesn't matter what William wants, his front right incisor is in need of some attention! Open up, Bill," he said advancing his fork towards William's mouth. "Let's have a look."

"Dad!" Eva cried.

"Eva, I merely want to help the boy! He clearly has issues with his dental hygiene."

"Benjamin!" Jennifer said sternly, her knife clattering against her plate.

Dr Poots seemed to wake suddenly at the noise and lowered his fork to the table.

"I'm… I'm sorry, William. I can't help it, you see.

Dentistry. I see a tooth in need of attention and it's my first instinct to try and fix it."

William did his best to laugh it off. "Not to worry, Ben. Not at all. I... fell out of a tree and chipped it. It was wet... raining... I've been meaning to get this tooth looked at for a long time, actually."

"Not that I was expecting you to look at it," he added quickly.

"Well that's settled then! I'll take a look after tea."

Before William could answer, Jennifer leaned towards him. "Pass me your plate, William darling."

Later, after the table had been cleared, Jennifer began rummaging through the fridge. "Who's for dessert?" she asked, emerging with a black forest gateau.

"Mmh," Ed mumbled.

"Yes please," Eva said.

"None for me, dear," Dr Poots said.

William was about to answer when Dr Poots turned to him. "You'd better not have anything sweet until I've taken a look at that tooth, William."

William opened and closed his mouth, then nodded weakly.

After watching everyone except Dr Poots eat their dessert, William thanked Mrs Poots for a lovely meal and helped her clear the table. Ed slinked off to his room and William was obliged to sit at the table while Jennifer and Eva enjoyed the largest coffees ever recorded. Dr Poots had long since made his excuses and gone off to some other section of the house that held more immediate interest.

It was just as William was hoping the last dregs of the coffee might be in sight when Dr Poots returned. He had rolled up the sleeves of a new shirt and was grinning in what William feared was macabre anticipation.

"Right, William. Everything's set up, come on. Let's get to know each other a bit." He gestured at William to get up and join him.

"Dad, please, we're having a conversation," Eva said and William became retrospectively aware that he had been engaged in a vague discussion about where he came from, who his family were, what he hoped to achieve from life.

"Darling, let William relax. He doesn't need to be subjected to your torture chair this evening."

All colour drained from William's face and ran down his back in the form of cold drops of sweat. "Torture chair?" he asked, injecting the words with his best attempt at humour.

"His dentist's chair," Eva said, rolling her eyes. "Dad, leave him alone."

"Eva, William here has the chance to get his tooth seen to by one of the best dentists in the country. He's not going to pass that up. Now, come on, William."

William smiled and glanced about the table. His grin slipped away as mother and daughter shrugged and William realised a dental probing was becoming a very real possibility.

"Right, that's settled that," Dr Poots said, placing a hand on William's shoulder.

William followed Dr Poots downstairs into a dark room that smelled strongly of disinfectant, like an operating theatre or a caretaker's closet. An electric light stuttered into life overhead then hummed along steadily. William glanced about as the room emerged around him. A dentist's chair of dry green leather was the centrepiece, surrounded by shelves and glass-fronted cupboards stuffed with jars, dusty manila files and yet more taxidermy. A wooden globe stood in a corner and William suddenly wished he was anywhere but there.

"Make yourself comfortable," Dr Poots said, nodding towards the chair. William laughed nervously, but the sound slowly dropped away inside his chest and he was left with no choice but to do as he was told. The chair was comfortable but as soon as he had positioned himself, Dr Poots advanced and flicked on a bright white light, which he angled carefully over William's face.

"Eva, if you wouldn't mind."

Out of the corner of his eye, William spotted Eva, the

girl who was possibly the love of his life, moving about amongst the shelves and cupboards, bringing forth glass jars of blue liquid. A goat's skull shone white in the dazzling glow. Eva placed a jar on the metal tray at her father's elbow and began removing metallic instruments. William noticed she was now clad in a pair of plastic gloves and a disposable plastic smock.

Jennifer was standing beside her, dressed in the same get-up and handing the metal instruments to her husband, one by one.

Before William had a chance to call out to Eva, to tell her that enough was enough and that he would make an appointment with his own dentist as soon as was humanly possible, Dr Poots' face appeared above him like that of a deity looking down from amongst the clouds.

"Open wide."

William opened his mouth and closed his eyes. He felt suddenly removed from what was going on. It was as if the entire situation was so surreal that it couldn't possibly be happening. If he could just close his eyes, it would all be over with and they could all go back to being a normal family, and him a normal boyfriend, all of them engaged in polite, normal conversation, him desperately trying not to inadvertently allude to the fact that he knew sex existed.

William's eyes might have been shut but his ears were not and it was hard to ignore the sound of Dr Poot's voice calling out numbers, declaring there was a fissure here, or a stain there. "Write that down, Eva," he was saying.

The sensation of the cold metal probe poking his teeth was amplified by William's temporary blindness and each jab and scrape felt like a personal attack. Worse was to come when Dr Poots turned his attention to William's chipped front tooth. To William, it felt as though his future father-in-law had hooked something blunt yet keen behind his tooth and was attempting to pull it apart with this device. William's hands slipped off the chair's arm rests.

"Stop squirming there, William. Open up a bit more. A bit more. That's it. That's it. Nearly got it."

The pain was almost unbearable now and William's eyes snapped open. Dr Poots loomed above him, his eyes wide and fixated, his nostril hairs shaking in a strong down draft. William closed his eyes again but the light that shone above him now seemed brighter than ever. Then, as quickly as the pain had begun, it ended. Dr Poots removed the instrument from his mouth and William's body went limp as a cold film of relief crept over him.

"Good news, William. It's nothing serious. You'll need a veneer. Usually quite expensive, but don't worry about that."

William opened his eyes tentatively. Dr Poots was standing some distance away, smiling down at him. Eva sat at a desk of brushed steel, writing something in a brown notebook.

"Yes, I'll fix you up tomorrow. Anyone who is all right with Eva is all right with me. Don't you worry about it, no money need exchange hands between family."

William felt the cold sweat evaporate. "Thank you…" he began but his tongue was dry. He swallowed and tried again. "Thank you very much, that's very kind of you… Ben."

"Not to worry, Bill. Not to worry."

William started laughing to himself. He couldn't help it. There had never been anything to be afraid of. He pushed himself up on his elbows and began to swing his legs out of the chair.

"Wait a moment, William!" Dr Poots cried, advancing towards him again. "We've still got work to do. We haven't had a look at those molars, yet."

William's eyes darted helplessly towards Eva. As if sensing him, she glanced up from her notebook and smiled. Afraid he was being childish again, William sat back down in the chair.

"Now open wide again, please," Dr Poots said, leaning over him.

Of course it was all right, William thought. Dr Poots was a fantastic man, offering to fix his tooth for free. He came on a little bit strong, but then there was nothing wrong with that, really.

"A bit wider, William."

William began to feel the instruments prodding his teeth. He kept his eyes open this time, staring up Dr Poots' nose; the absurdity of this view giving him something else to focus on. His tongue was upsetting the probe. A frown creased Dr Poot's brow. William closed his eyes and decided not to worry. He was a real character – an eccentric, you might say, but a good man nonetheless. Everything was all right. He had found a good family.

A sharp nudge interrupted his train of thought and a jolt of pain travelled down into his gum. "Oww," he said around the cold metal probe.

He was expecting a laugh or an apology and when none came he opened his eyes. Dr Poots was leaning closer than ever and William could feel his warm breath against his cheek and eyes.

"This won't do at all. Not at all. There's only one thing to be done. Eva, fetch the gas."

"What?" William cried.

"One of your molars is in a terrible state, William. It's all but rotted away. It's on the verge of disintegration. I'm afraid if we don't act now you'll be at a terrible risk of gum disease."

Eva came over, wheeling a thin, grey cylinder towards them, the wheels squeaking with each revolution.

"What's that in aid of?" William gasped, pushing himself up from the chair.

"Now, don't worry, son. It'll all be over soon. We'll get you sorted out." Dr Poots smiled, his hand resting firmly on William's shoulder.

Jennifer appeared above him and pressed his shoulders down into the chair, a flick of blue paint on the underside of her chin. "Just relax," she whispered.

"It's OK. It doesn't matter. Honestly," William spluttered from around Dr Poots' gloved fingers."

A rubber mask came into view, a dark triangle against

the light, and then it descended and filled his vision. The light shining down on him became dim, making William feel as though he were drunk. Time passed in slow motion as William became numb to the feel of Dr Poots' elbows in his ribs. The last thing he saw before the darkness came over him was Eva smiling down at him, with love in her eyes.

The Intern and The Exploding Magazine

Six pm Friday and it was all over. Larry did the rounds, shaking the hands of everyone in the office.

"Hey Jack, don't forget that haircut! What? Ha-ha yeah, you too man…You too."

"Hey, Alice, if only we worked together more often, eh? Ha-ha. Maybe, baby."

Handshakes. Thanks and good luck. Good work but still no job for you!

Larry didn't mind. Not really. It was a lot of fun, all these internships. It was great; he was getting to try out working at all these magazines that he would never have even dreamed of working at, never have imagined himself working at. Never really wanted to work at. But it was the way into the industry, and he got all of this experience for free.

It was Oscar's last day there as well and they stood now by the elevator, not free but not quite part of the office. They stood awkwardly watching the elevator numbers light up while everyone who actually worked at the magazine worked on as though they weren't there. Oscar was looking bloody stylish, Larry thought. He was wearing his Ramones t-shirt. Larry had been about to put his Ramones t-shirt on that morning but he'd gone for his Sonic Youth t-shirt instead. How wrong he had been. Oscar looked pretty damn stylish. His hair was slicked back and he had those circular sunglasses on that everyone was wearing these days. Larry would have to get some, maybe look down Kingsland Road over the weekend.

He'd never really been a fan of Oscar. There was something about him… something a bit… stuck up. That was the phrase. Besides, they had been rivals. Larry had been on Oscar's trail across London over the past few months, from magazine to magazine, like rival archaeologists, dashing about Egypt after ancient treasure. Or spies running across Poland after secret Soviet papers. Or interns after a job. Still, the battle (but not the war) was over and now there was time for some interaction. Christmas football in the trenches.

"So," Larry began, but just then the elevator arrived and they stepped in together. "So,' he began again, "that went well eh? What are you up to now? Fancy a pint? Bloody deserve it, eh?"

Oscar lifted his trendy glasses and rubbed beneath them for a moment before letting them fall back into place. "Can't I'm afraid," he said, staring straight ahead.

"But it's Saturday tomorrow!" Larry said and he cursed himself for sounding so disappointed.

"You're right," Oscar said. "But I'm starting work. Finally got a *job*."

"A job?" Larry asked. His palms became clammy and the temperature in the elevator rose ten degrees.

"Yup, all these internships have finally paid off."

"It's at a newspaper?" Larry asked trying to remember which titles Oscar had worked at. Before Oscar himself could answer Larry cut in, "No, a magazine. It's a magazine?"

Oscar sighed and nodded his head almost imperceptibly, "Correct."

"Where? *Esquire*? *GQ*? Not fucking *Vice*? It's fucking *Vice* isn't it?"

The elevator doors opened and Oscar hurried out. Larry ran to keep up.

"You're working at *Vice*, aren't you?"

Larry knew he should have bought some of those sunglasses. He'd been a fool not to.

"It… it's a new magazine," Oscar said almost nervously as he held the door open for Larry.

"What's it called?"

48

"You won't have heard of it."

"Oh, come on! Help a pal out!"

Oscar let go of the door handle and stepped back into the foyer. He lifted his shades and glanced furtively from side to side. "OK, it's… it's a new magazine… an exploding magazine."

"Cool man, it's blowing up, eh?" Larry nodded enthusiastically while his stomach churned with jealousy. "So, what's it called?"

"No one knows," Oscar whispered.

"Oh cool… erm, what?" Larry scratched his chin.

Oscar stepped closer.

"Well, no one knows because… like I said, it's an exploding magazine."

Oscar waited for a look of understanding on Larry's face. When none was forthcoming he continued, "It's not technically an *exploding* magazine, it's more… well, it's such a fucking cool magazine, it's so totally *amazeballs* that whoever reads it, their heads literally explode. That's why no one knows its name."

Larry rubbed his eyes and then laughed, before stopping and leaning in closer to Oscar.

"Seriously?" he whispered.

"Deadly," Oscar said. "Dick put me in touch with it."

"'Dick?"

"Dick. From *Splendid Homes Magazine*."

"Oh. Dick."

"Yes. You can't breathe a word to anyone. Obviously it's an incredibly sensitive issue. No one can find out, or there'd be country-wide deaths. People's minds being blown left, right and centre, and after that, where's your readership gone?"

"I don't know? Dead?"

"Dead. Blown to fucking smithereens."

Larry nodded. "I won't tell anyone. But how do people know they have the right magazine?"

"I've heard – mind you I haven't actually seen it – I've heard the front cover is always inside a black plastic bag, so no one can read it. Not even the title. I've heard that's the most dangerous part."

A car passed by outside and Oscar suddenly made for the door. "I have to go. It was nice knowing you. Don't pursue this, will you?"

"Yeah... Of course I won't," Larry said as Oscar stepped out into the sunlight.

"You bastard," Larry thought. "I'm going to blow this thing wide open!"

Larry hurried out into the street and glanced left and right, but there was no sign of Oscar.

***

Larry was distracted the entire journey home. An exploding magazine. Or, rather, a magazine that blew people's heads apart like bloody ripe melons. Jesus. He thought he'd seen it all, or rather *heard* it all. He'd done seven internships now. *Seven.* He'd run across London with burgers that promised they were the spiciest thing in the world. He'd shot super-soakers off roofs at unsuspecting pedestrians. He'd transcribed interviews about cats with famous actors. He'd been in the same rooms as C list celebrities. He'd drunk shots of different mouthwashes until he was sick (he still couldn't pick a winner). He'd eaten pack after pack of chocolate liqueurs until he was sick again. He'd kissed arse until the taste of shit was permanently in his mouth, and all the mouthwashes in the world couldn't help him.

The only bit of luck he had had was an article he'd written for a women's magazine on giving the perfect blow job. He'd written it under the pseudonym 'Sue D'Nimm'. Larry had decided she was a Korean immigrant and a fiend for cock and he had got paid a hundred quid. He'd used his own experiences as a heterosexual male and reversed them to give every girl a brilliant, foolproof guide. And all the while they were completely unaware that these vivid insights really came from a chap's point of view.

He hadn't told his father about that one. Every week he

would call and ask what Larry had been doing and if he had a job yet. Larry had been able to appease him with the occasional article on a magazine's website, but now he was running out of his father's money and any hint of the blow job story was sure to blow his cash flow as well as his already strained relationship with the old boy.

As soon as Larry got in he fired up his laptop, moved it across to the window, put the kettle on, made a green tea and changed into his fucking Ramones t-shirt. Then he opened his emails. No job offers or acceptances, or even rejections of freelance articles. It had been a slow day. Slow week. He opened his address book and scoured the names for those who might know about this exploding magazine and added them all into an email. He typed out the message asking for information, reminding them who he was. He was about to hit send when he stopped and deleted the whole thing.

Jesus. What was he doing? If he sent this email out to all these people, every one of his competitors would know about the exploding magazine. Oscar had said to keep it secret, but more importantly, tipping off these bastards at other magazines was clearly going to ensure one of those slimy bloody toads would steal the story for themselves. Larry had to keep it secret. Sub rosa. Mum's the word. He drew up a new email and selected only 'Dick- Splendid Homes Magazine' and sent it off to him.

For an hour Larry sat intently at his desk, waiting for a reply. At one point the phone rang and Larry ran to it, tripping over the chair to answer it. It was only his mother wishing him well. Larry slammed the phone down.

His girlfriend, Mary, arrived home shortly afterwards.

"'How was your last day, babe? Did they offer you a job?" she asked, taking off her coat.

"No, they bloody didn't," Larry replied.

He looked her up and down and decided he could trust her. He reached out a hand and pulled her to him.

"Ooh, Larry!' she giggled.

"What? Shut up and listen, Mary," he said. He

recounted the conversation he'd had with Oscar, finishing in a whisper and looking about the room as though expecting to see electronic bugs hidden behind a photo frame or nestling on top of a plant pot.

"I don't believe it," Mary said as, with a shake of her head, she jumped up from Larry's lap and went off to make some food.

Larry stared after her, dumbstruck.

***

Later Larry stood by the window looking out over the city bathed in orange light. People moved about beneath him and not one of them knew about the magazine. They couldn't or their heads wouldn't be intact. But someone, somewhere, must know. Someone knew. Someone had kept their head, after all, who had given that prick Oscar his job? Someone. Mary stirred in the bed and woke up.

"Larry. Come back to bed," she purred.

Larry climbed back in beside her, her nipples erect in the half light.

"I can't bloody sleep," he said, flicking at the nearest nipple. It bounced back and he flicked it again.

"Stop it, Larry. Stop it," Mary said, pulling the cover up around her tits.

"I can't. I *need* to find this magazine. My career depends on it."

"No, I meant stop flicking my—"

Suddenly Larry's laptop screen lit up and there was the ping of received mail.

"Shut up!" Larry said.

He jumped out of bed and ran to the laptop. The message was from Dick at *Splendid Homes Magazine*.

Dear whomever you are, This sounds like the biggest load of nonsense ever. I have not heard of this magazine. I categorically deny any involvement with such an absurd notion. Any further

enquiries can be taken up with my lawyer. Until then,
   Please fuck off and kill yourself."

Fondest,
Dick - Splendid Homes Magazine

"Aha!" Larry cried, jumping in triumph.

"What?" Mary asked, half asleep.

"Come and read this. Come and bloody read this!" he said, jabbing a finger at the screen. "He all but admits it! The cat's out of the bag. I'm gonna blow this thing wide open and then I'll be able to get a job anywhere!"

But Mary had already gone back to sleep.

***

Larry was unable to sleep, then, suddenly, it was morning. Saturday and nothing to do. He remembered the email, jumped out of bed and read it through four times. Then he sent an email back to Dick: wink wink, nudge nudge, let's meet up and talk about it. Mary had already gone to work so there was nothing else to do except go out and look for inspiration. Sometimes, *just sometimes,* if Larry let his mind wander he could walk around, *seemingly* at random, but come across some monumental clue as to what he should do next. Usually, it was located in the Cafe Nero at the end of the road, but today he felt some deeper inspiration coming on.

He set off after another half an hour and began his search. He wandered through Regent's Park. He found young couples in the sun, but no evidence there. No sign of any magazines in black packages. Or exploded heads. He headed into a newsagent and stared for a long time at the magazines on the top shelf in their plastic wrappers. After ten minutes the man behind the counter asked him to leave. It's a bloody ruse, Larry thought. This guy is in on it! He was about to tear down the magazines and rip open their covers when a police car cruised past outside.

Larry narrowed his eyes at the shopkeeper as he left, "That's just not cricket, mate."

Larry bought a pack of cigarettes at a different newsagent and stood smoking them while scowling out across the Thames from London Bridge, narrowing his eyes as he took a drag, trying not to cough.

For lunch he met Mary outside a cafe but was unable to concentrate on anything she said.

"You're not listening to me!" she said. "And, when did you start smoking?"

Larry laughed. "Mary, I started smoking this morning. I can't very well listen to you with all this hanging over me, now can I?"

Mary looked towards the heavens and spoke quietly under her breath.

Larry rolled his eyes and stood up. "I have to go. I'll see you at home."

"Oh, all right," she said but Larry was already gone.

***

When Mary returned from work Larry was sitting by the window looking out at the evening sky, dressed in trousers, a vest and a fedora, rubbing his temple as he chain-smoked cigarettes.

"What's with the hat, Dick Tracy?" Mary asked.

"Yes, exactly. You need a hat if you're going to be a private dick."

"I thought you wanted to be a journalist?"

Larry took a drag on his cigarette. He took it from his mouth, pinched it between his fingers and looked at it with narrowed eyes. By now he'd practised doing this to perfection.

"It's the same thing, baby," he said, his voice husky.

"Oh, Larry!" Mary said as Larry carried her off to bed.

Larry awoke suddenly some hours later to a beeping in the darkness. He sat up in a daze. It was the phone. He ran out of bed and tore it from the wall. He sat on the floor and held it to his ear, as he usually did when speaking on the phone.

"Larry Kuntz?" A deep, growling, menacing voice asked.

"Yes, this is he. I mean, yes it's me, I'm him."

The voice on the other end was overtaken by a fit of coughing. Suddenly it became a high-pitched, slightly effeminate voice with a Lancashire accent.

"Oooh, sorry mate, bloody sore throat. Too many fags."

Larry stumped out his newly lit cigarette on the floor.

"I've heard you're after some information about..." and here the voice lowered until it was almost inaudible, "...the exploding magazine."

Larry gulped. "Erm, yes... yes... please," he whispered back.

"Speak up, lad!" the voice boomed. "I can hardly hear you."

"Sorry. Is this... is this Dick?" Larry asked at a reasonable volume.

"No. Handjob."

"No handjob? Erm I... I didn't want... I... just wanted to know about the magazine..."

The voice on the other end continued, "You call me 'Handjob'. It's a code name, a whatdyacallit?"

"Sue D'Nimm." Larry said.

"Who?"

"Yeah, code name," Larry said.

"Look, I can't speak now, but meet me tomorrow in Debenhams – in the cafe – and we'll have a chat."

"Debenhams?"

"Yeah, it's got clothes and all sorts, furniture I think. One of them department stores. The wife's always off down Debenhams. But it's a good place for a meet. Nice and public, like."

"I see. Shall we say two?"

"Can't do two, got the dentists at one, might run over. Maybe three?"

"OK, how will I recognise you?"

"You won't. I'll recognise you. I've been following you on Twitter for quite some time. Don't worry about that."

"OK," Larry said.

"You need directions to Debenhams?"

"No, it's… it's just inside the shopping centre right? Second floor… next to…"

"That's the one. Now, keep it secret." And the voice rang off.

Larry paced the room in excitement. He was on the trail, he could smell the scent. The pig was in the poke. The lion leaps at midnight. But he was also suspicious, least of all about a dental appointment on a Sunday. You never knew who you could trust, least of all in this business.

***

The next day Larry woke at seven a.m. He rolled over and looked at the clock.

"Fuck that," he said and went back to bed until about one twenty-five.

He woke up and had a shower, a green tea and some toast. Mary was still bloody sleeping. He dressed quickly and slid a kitchen knife into his jacket pocket. Best be bloody careful. If they were making a magazine that exploded people's heads, who knew what they would do to someone asking the wrong questions? Anything, was what.

Larry arrived at Debenhams and scouted out the joint. Queer looking customers, every bloody one of them. Not a soul to be trusted. He couldn't find his man, though. He sat for an hour in the cafe and had a coffee, then a tea, then another coffee, but still no one approached him. After another fifteen minutes he decided to give up, and left.

Larry was disappointed but there was a new Xbox game he wanted and he knew picking it up while he was in the area would cheer him up. It would be quicker to go out through the multi-storey car-park, then he could go to HMV and buy it, or failing that, Argos, he decided.

The car park was dark and stank of spilt petrol. Larry

weaved his way amongst the cars, cutting through to the exit on the opposite side. A light flickered by the door then died, leaving Larry in darkness. Suddenly, to his left, Larry became aware of a figure standing in the shadows. He grasped the knife in his pocket, just in case. The figure was a man in a long trench coat with a hat pulled down low over his eyes. He stared at Larry intently.

"Erm... Handjob?" Larry asked.

"Please!" the man cried, throwing open his trench coat to reveal a pink and naked body beneath. He advanced towards Larry, his penis flapping from side to side. Larry forgot the knife and ran for his life.

He was almost out of the car park when he ran slap-bang into a man's back. The man turned, a bloody handkerchief held to his mouth. He was in his forties and dressed in a purple pinstripe suit.

"Bloody heck! Larry!" he said then held out his hand along with the bloody 'kerchief.

"Oops, sorry," he said, swapping that hand for his other while he stuffed the handkerchief up his sleeve. His mouth looked slightly swollen on one side.

"Dentists," he said, raising his eyebrows.

"Handjob?" Larry asked.

"That's me." The man shook Larry's hand enthusiastically. "Now," he said, looking around conspiringly, "what do you want to know?"

"Well," Larry whispered. "What can you tell me about the magazine?"

"A lot," Handjob said. "I started the damn thing. Oscar said you were after some information, well I've got the dope!"

"Dope!" Larry said, his eyes wide.

"The dope, the skinny, the information." Handjob smiled.

"Oh." Larry nodded. "Give it to me, Handjob."

"Well," Handjob said, pausing to check their surroundings once more. "It all began in Williamsburg, Brooklyn in 1976..."

Half an hour later, Larry shook Handjob's hand. Tracking him down had been a job well done. He was pleased with the results. Now he had everything he needed to know, straight from the horse's mouth!

"Well goodbye then, and thanks a million!" Larry said.

"Hold on!" Handjob said,

"Before you go…" He turned and rummaged through the rubbish in the front seat of his car.

Larry's heart began to thunder in his chest and he gripped the knife in his jacket pocket once more.

Handjob emerged from the car with a brown paper bag. "I want you to have this," he said, handing the bag to Larry.

Larry let go of the knife and took the package. Slowly, he looked inside. There, right in front of him, was what looked to be a magazine wrapped in black plastic.

"Take a look," Handjob said. "But don't read it. We'd like you alive. We want you to be part of our team. You've shown some inventiveness, son. Initiative. Pep. Well done." He pumped Larry's hand in his again.

"Take a while to think about it. My email's on the first page. Now I've got to go and wash my mouth out with bloody salt water. See you soon!"

Handjob turned, got into his car, struggled with the ignition, then drove away, leaving Larry in a cloud of smoke. Larry leaned back on the bonnet of a Vauxhall Astra and glanced carefully at the package in his hands. Well, you didn't look a gift horse in the mouth…

***

He ran home, the magazine hidden inside his jacket like a banned book, feeling like a pervert hiding women's lingerie beneath a trench coat. When he got home it was raining and his hair was plastered to his face. He ran into the flat. Mary was out. He threw his clothes on the floor. The paper bag that held the magazine was soaked and falling apart. Feeling a cold coming on, Larry threw the magazine onto the bed and went to take a shower.

An hour later he sat staring at the magazine in its dark plastic wrapper. Was it a trap? What if it wasn't the right magazine? What if he opened it, read it, and his head didn't explode? He would know he had been duped. The police would probably burst in, pointing rifles and arrest him for journalistic espionage. Or worse. Handjob and Oscar would get hold of him together. He might disappear for good. Speaking of which, Mary was still not back...

Larry stood up and crossed to the window. In the rain he swore he could see a car idling by the curve below. Jesus. They were watching him. They probably had his place under surveillance. He had to get out, lie low. He took the magazine and slid it under the mattress. He needed some sort of disguise... some way to get out of there without anyone recognising him.

Twenty minutes later he left the flat in an obscure collection of his own clothes and Mary's. He had one of her skirts wrapped around his head, his fedora resting on top. He'd even put on a bit of her make-up; lots of foundation so he didn't look like the skinny white boy he was. He made his way downstairs, nodding to those he passed, putting on a strange and invented accent.

"Helluh," he said to a woman who put her hands over her children's eyes and hurried them onwards.

When Larry got outside the car had gone. Still, there might be other agents lurking around. Who could tell? For an hour he did a lap of the block, getting gradually wetter until he decided to nip into a cafe for a coffee. He sat down but left four minutes later, pursued by the hysterical cries of a group of teenage girls.

Round and round he walked, aimlessly in the rain. His hat was soggy and the foundation ran in great splodges down his cheeks. There had been no sign of anyone following him, but then a good spy never left a trail. He sat on a park bench and a dog ran up and barked at him before being torn away by its owner – a short, squat man who glared at him in disgust.

"Come away, Finn! Come away!"

This was no sort of life, Larry thought. If this was what fame, fortune and respect cost, it wasn't worth it. He was out. Besides, he was hungry. He hadn't eaten anything since breakfast, except for a Snickers before he'd gone in Debenhams. He hadn't been about to buy anything in there. Jesus Christ. With those prices? He was no mug.

Larry made his way home. On the stairs he took off the fedora and Mary's blouse and wiped his face with her skirt before stuffing it into a bin. He put the hat back on. He hoped she wouldn't think he had been stupid. He hoped she'd cooked him his tea. He fancied fried eggs, maybe some smiley faces.

Larry struggled to get the key in the lock, his fingers slippery and wet. In a second he would be warm and safe inside. The door opened. He stepped in then closed the door behind him and flicked on the lights. Someone had decorated. Stripes and splashes of red covered the walls and even the duvet. There was Mary (finally), knelt on the floor by the bed.

Something dropped from the ceiling. It was a fleshy scrap of scalp that had been stuck up there like a pancake. It flopped down and landed on Larry's shoe, shiny with blood. He looked around the room once more. Scraps of skull and brain decorated the walls and the counter tops. A scrap of hair had landed on his laptop, he noticed with annoyance. That would be hell to get off. Oh, bloody hell though, Mary!

He knelt beside Mary at the side of the bed, and sure enough, she was missing the top half of her head. Her mind had been blown. All that was left was a bloody stump where the top of her neck had been. Oh, Jesus, what had he done? What could he do now?

Larry glanced around. There was something in Mary's hands, something magazine-shaped. He hadn't noticed the black plastic wrapper discarded on the bed, hidden as it was under pints of wet blood. His eyes swept over the magazine in Mary's hands. He tried not to read, but he couldn't help but catch a few words. Before Larry could do anything about it, there was a crack and the sound of a balloon popping or ripe fruit squashing underfoot and then a sudden rain of red liquid fell from the air before a splattered fedora floated down onto the bed.

***

Outside in his car Oscar lowered his binoculars. He picked up his phone and dialled a number. Someone answered.

"Got the bastard," he said. Then he hung up and drove away.

The Brothers

Pandora reached between her legs and when she brought her hand away the tips of her fingers were red.

"Hmm."

She wiped her fingers on the bathroom towel. She knew what to do and where her mother kept her own things and she opened the cupboard and took the box down.

When she left the bathroom a few minutes later her mother almost ran into her.

"Pandora, where have you been? You can't disappear on your birthday!"

"I'm right here," Pandora said.

Her mother seemed not to hear, but took her by the hand and led her into the lounge where children were sitting at the table in party hats, pink plastic plates in front of them.

"Go sit down," her mother said, nodding towards the empty place at the head of the table.

Pandora walked the length of the room, passing the adults who stood leaning against chairs and cabinets with their drinks in hand, awaiting the start of the birthday dinner.

Her father's brothers stood there, each with a glass of whisky, and as she passed they whistled and said things like, "There she goes, the most beautiful girl in the world" and "Hard to believe she's only twelve!"

Pandora shivered and tried to pull her dress further down over her thighs. She could feel their eyes on her, as though her body had sent a signal to all of the men in the room that she was a woman now and was ready when they were.

"Pandora! Sit down!" her mother shouted.

Pandora took her place. She glanced down the length of the table at the collection of school friends and younger cousins chattering to each other in their pink dresses, cardigans and bow ties. Suddenly, they all seemed much too young to be there.

Her youngest cousin poked himself in the nose with his plastic spoon and started to cry. Pandora looked around at the adults on the fringes of the table. They were all too busy with each other to notice what the children were doing. Their jaws hung as loosely as their children's, and they squawked with laughter and swayed on their feet as they drank their drinks.

Only Pandora's uncles seemed to be paying any attention, looking at her over the rims of their glasses, huddled together in the shadows behind the lamp.

"OK, everyone!" Pandora's mother shouted as she burst back into the room, a cake balanced before her.

The lights dimmed and a chorus of "Happy Birthday" started up. Pandora watched, bored, as the cake made its way down the table, shimmering in candlelight.

"Here you are!" her mother cried as she set the cake down.

Before she was halfway through saying, "Make a wish!" Pandora had blown the candles out, showering the cake in flecks of spittle, the candles standing drunkenly in the pink icing.

"Pandora!" her mother hissed. "You're supposed to wait. We'll have to do it again!"

"I'm not doing it again."

"You'll do as you're told."

"I'm not fucking doing it again," Pandora said and her mother whispered through gritted teeth. "Don't start all this, you ungrateful bitch."

"I'm not a child, I'm twelve years old," Pandora said, noticing a rim of blood beneath her middle finger nail.

She dipped her bloody finger into the cake and brought it away with a huge mound of pink icing resting atop it. She slid the finger into her mouth and sucked the icing away, the faint taste of blood mingling with the sickly flavour of the icing. She glanced at her uncles and saw them gulp uncomfortably.

She stood up to leave the table.

Her mother was still standing beside her when Pandora hissed, "I never wanted a fucking pink cake."

After dinner the children were playing in the garden, watched over by the adults who had by now descended into drunkenness and were parodying their games. There was an extra edge to the adult's games. Hands lingered longer than they should, elbows met breasts and were drawn away without apologies and neighbours clashed together at the hips with cries of, "Oops! How many have I had?"

Pandora left the garden and made her way through the quiet corridors of the house. There was no chance of getting any alcohol from the table. The adults guarded it like treasure, but Pandora knew where her mother's secret stash was and she made her way through the house towards it.

As she passed the bathroom, she heard a strange gasping noise, like from someone in pain. She crept to the door and placed her eye against the keyhole. Her uncle Norm stood facing her, his eyes shut and his head tilted back. He didn't appear to be in pain. In fact, he looked as if he was putting a great deal of effort into concentrating on something. The back of Pandora's mother's head moved slowly in front of his crotch, her hands rubbing up and down on his trousers, while his hands fed through her red hair.

Pandora turned away from the door. Something was happening in her stomach. She was about to turn back to the keyhole when her second uncle, Pete, came down the corridor, treading uncertainly as though the floor was tilting beneath him. When he saw Pandora standing there, alone in the corridor, he stopped for a brief second, then came towards her more steadily.

"Hello beauty," he said. "Have you seen Norm?"

"No, Uncle Pete," she said, swallowing to get rid of the taste in her mouth.

"Well…if you see him, tell him – Norm that is – that I

was looking for him," he said.

His moustache twitched of its own accord as if a big caterpillar that slept there was just waking up.

They stood like that for a second, Pandora blocking the hallway.

Finally she said, "What do you want him for?"

"Who? Oh, Norm. Oh, nothing important," he said, taking a drink from the plastic cup in his hand before scratching his head and glancing about uneasily.

Pandora came closer, her nose almost touching his fat stomach and then, as she had seen her mother do, she placed a hand on her uncle's leg.

"Do you think I could have some of that… Pete?" she asked in a voice made of innocence and sweets.

Her uncle stood stock still as though moving might cause the world to end.

"What?" he asked quietly.

"The drink," Pandora said, keeping her hand where it was.

"It's not for girls… erm, I mean children," he said and his moustache twitched again.

"But it's my birthday," Pandora whined. "Please."

Pete looked around quickly. No one was about. "OK, have a quick drink, but then I have to go."

He handed her the glass like it was something he wanted to get rid of. Pandora took it in both hands and thought she heard Pete sigh as her hand left his leg. She took a long drink of the whisky. Her throat burned and her head felt light. A drop escaped over her lips and she stuck her tongue out and caught it with the rounded tip and then the tongue slid back into her mouth. She handed the glass back.

Pete took it quickly, then looked about again.

"OK. Well, Happy Birthday, young lady!"

He made to squeeze past her, but Pandora was already slipping past him in the opposite direction.

"Thanks, Uncle Pete!" she winked up at him, and when she glanced back he was still watching her, and taking a long drink on the last of his whisky.

The rain came down in great sheets, compounding the misery of the mourners who huddled beneath large black umbrellas. They lowered the coffin into the ground and the priest read another prayer as they stood with bowed heads. Pandora stood at the front in her black dress, her leather jacket over her shoulders. The rain darkened her peroxide hair and pasted it to her neck.

"Come under the umbrella," her mother hissed.

Pandora ignored her.

She glanced around at the faces of the mourners. Her family was there but her grandparents had refused to come. A suicide didn't get into heaven and they wanted no part in seeing their sinful son descend into hell. Only her mother's mother stood there, frail in her black shawl, head bent to the ground.

Amongst the sodden rows of mourners, there was only one other person who held their head high. Norm, greying now, glared across at his niece and moved his jaw slowly as though chewing on a bit of gristle stuck amongst his teeth. Pandora met his gaze and smiled with her thick red lips. Norm took a step forward and the priest looked up, momentarily faltering in his prayer. Norm shook his head and disappeared through the crowd and away.

Afterwards, as made their way to the waiting cars, Pandora's father came jogging across to her and her mother.

"Have you seen my brother?" he asked. "Norm, I mean. Well, my brother."

Pandora's mother shook her head. "No, but if you see him you'd be wise to keep him away from me. And this one," she said, nodding at Pandora.

"He's just upset. He doesn't mean it," Pandora's father said. He wrinkled his nose as a trickle of rain ran down it.

"I won't have it, Bill," Pandora's mother said. "I won't have your brother accusing our daughter. She's fifteen years old, for God's sake. Your brother was ill, and that's no fault

66

of hers. She's... she's the one who was hurt."

Pandora's father pushed his wet hair away from his forehead. "I know, dear, I know. But..." he said, glancing at Pandora. "But... Norm does have a right to be here. I just wanted to speak to him. Pete was his brother too, after all. We've only got each other now."

"Well go find him then," Pandora's mother said.

Pandora's father walked off in the rain calling out his brother's name.

Pandora walked with her mother for a few moments. She couldn't help but laugh quietly.

Her mother grabbed her by the arms and turned her round to face her. "I don't know what you're laughing at," she hissed.

"Oh sod off, mum. He was a sick old man, you know that. You know what him and Norm were like, don't you?" Pandora said with a flicker of a smile on her face.

"You're a bitch," her mother said. "You're not wearing that leather jacket to the wake. It looks scruffy. I can't believe you wore it to the funeral. Dressing like that, there's no wonder..."

"I'm not going to the wake," Pandora said.

"We'll see about that."

"We will," Pandora said as she hitched up her dress and slipped off into the bushes, her mother's cries echoing after her.

Rain made its way down through the maze of branches as Pandora clomped through the mud, her black dress snagging on branches as she passed. She pushed through the bushes, casting about for something, and then, finally, she came upon the two boys huddled together, shivering and trying to stay out of the rain.

"Hello boys," she said as they crouched, trying not to let their teeth chatter as they shook with the cold. "Smile, you pussies. Do you have them?"

One of the boys wordlessly pulled a plastic sandwich bag from his pocket and held it out.

Pandora stuck her nose into the bag and inhaled deeply.

Then she reached inside and took one of the tightly rolled joints.

"My cousin got it for us," the second boy said as he fumbled with a lighter, before offering Pandora the flame.

Pandora batted his hand away and tossed the joint back into the bag with the others.

"Not here! I've just come from my uncle's funeral. Christ."

She placed a hand on each boy's chest and shoved them gently. "Let's go somewhere a bit more private."

She slid between them and pushed on through the undergrowth, the boys following her in the rain.

Persian Rugs

The house is swarming with people, creeping from one room to the next like lethargic slugs. A lot of them are people you do not know. The people you do know are not necessarily the people you had really wanted to turn up. There are not many girls here, but that can be dealt with later. What matters now is eliciting some drugs from the boy in the red Starter cap.

This guy is a friend of a friend of a friend. Tied on to your party like an escape rope made of bedding. And, like this rope, he is helping each of you to escape from your minds with his little bag of powders.

"Look," you say, "I don't mind you selling it, but this is our house so..."

The boy is slow. You don't know his name. His skin is the colour of greaseproof paper, and equally translucent. His veins throb beneath the skin, weirdly green and blue. His eyes are narrow with drooping lids and they do not look at you when you speak to him.

"Yeah...it is our house so...."

Still this boy does not understand. Or perhaps he does. His only response is to shuffle his feet back and forth on the fag-burned carpet while staring at the tip of his nose.

"Let's have a free sample, then," you say, exasperated at the length of time this is taking. If this guy wants to turn up to your house and deal drugs, the least he can do is offer them about.

Your housemate jokes that you're all in a gang called —. It's a joke, but also, not really. You believe that the two of you think this is true to some extent, and if some trouble were to arise, you could handle it. Luckily, this is not the

69

occasion for trouble. There have been other occasions on nights like this, occasions that have ended in cuts and bruises and terrible feelings of remorse the following day.

Tonight, the toady boy with the red hat tips the smallest amount of white powder into a square of cigarette rolling paper and wraps it up like a butcher wrapping up meat. He hands you the paper. This is called a bomb. It is ingested and as soon as the paper hits your stomach acid, the drug will start to fizz inside of you. Then your fingers will tickle and mischief will vibrate outwards from your heart. Your brain will also hover an inch or so above your head for the next two to three hours.

"Enjoy," the guy says, still not meeting your eyes.

Instead, he is grinning at the floor, as though this has been a great victory for him. It has not. It has been your victory, you tell yourself, as your mouth begins to twitch into a smile.

The boy shuffles off and you amble up the stairs where you pass your best friend and housemate, Sean. Sean is flanked by his friends from home. The whole group appears to be moving in slow motion and they reek of marijuana. As you pass them, you and Sean wink at each other, nodding slowly.

You are upstairs and your legs are moving of their own accord. There is a beautiful Lithuanian girl here tonight. Her name is Maria, and she is something like a *Playboy* cover star. You wonder if all Lithuanians are made like this. Your friend, Frankie lives with her. Bastard. You spot Frankie coming along the corridor. He bounds over and shakes your hand, his eyes wide like a puppy's.

"All right, mate!" he says. It is not a question. Rather, a statement that everything is good.

"Yes," you say, glancing around at the strangers stumbling along the corridor.

"Where's Maria?" you ask.

"She's here somewhere!" Frankie says, still gripping your hand.

"I'll find her," you say, turning to leave.

"Hang on!" Frankie says. He still has hold of your hand and he spins you back round.

"I didn't tell you, did I?"

"How do I know?" you say, suddenly giggling, suddenly feeling that everything is exactly how it should be.

"The other day, I left the flat and Maria was in on her own..." Frankie begins. He pauses for dramatic effect, his black eyebrows jumping excitedly.

"Go on," you say around a permanent grin.

"Well, I forgot my bag, so I went in and...."

"Spill the fucking beans!" you say.

"Well, Maria was about to get in the shower, and she just had this tiny towel held up in front of her! When I came in she smiled at me, then turned around and went into the bathroom. I just stood and watched her naked arse bob away!" Frankie says, biting his lip and rolling his eyes towards the ceiling, as though he is melting.

This story is almost too much. You are happy for Frankie, but it has not done anything for your confidence. Maria is a goddess, and you are only a mortal, if that. You are about to pump Frankie for more information (WHAT DOES HER ARSE LOOK LIKE?) when his girlfriend comes over and pulls him away. His lips snap shut like a guilty laptop screen.

"See you later," you say.

You wink, but are worried the wink is somehow sloppy and does not look cool. With Frankie's girlfriend is an Italian girl they know named Caterina. Caterina is OK-looking; in fact you nearly kissed her once at a party at Frankie's house. However, she is not quite Maria.

Later, you are sitting cross-legged on the faux-Persian rug in your bedroom. Maria and a few others are lounging around, smoking cigarettes. You do not smoke, but when Maria asked if it was OK, you could not refuse her. You are sitting on a collection of cushions and your white fairy lights bathe the room in a dull melancholy. The drug is wearing off and it feels like this might be the last night of your lives. But then, don't we die a little bit each day?

Maria is not interested in anything you have to say. You try to show her your bandaged finger. You cut it just before the party and had to rush off to A&E, you tell her. You could see the bone, but it's OK, you say.

Maria nods, then turns and speaks in some foreign language (most definitely Lithuanian) to her friend. They both tilt their heads back and roar with laughter. Maria's thick black hair shakes against her back.

When you had sawn down to the bone of your left forefinger while excitedly making a sandwich, you had been sure you would not make the party. Oh, it's fine, you thought at first, but then blood suddenly welled up in the narrow cut, and after you sucked the blood away, you looked down and saw white, gleaming bone. You and two of your flatmates had waited for the taxi to take you to the hospital, you pacing back and forth in the kitchen, white as a sheet, according to Sean.

The drugs are wearing away and Maria and her friends leave your bedroom. You are alone with the fairy lights. You sit and stare at them for a moment or two, then trudge downstairs. Everyone is gathered around in the living room. The boy with the blue veins and red hat is handing out balloons that he has filled with nitrous oxide. Mark, another one of your housemates, is sitting beside him, being offered free balloon, after free balloon. When, an hour ago, and in the middle of your MDMA high, you had wandered into the kitchen, Mark had been making pancakes, sober, as destruction rained about him. He had not seemed like he wanted to talk about how beautiful life was, as he flipped his pancakes amongst debris of flour and eggshells.

You watch Mark now, inhaling the gas. "Fuck off Mark", you think.

After a few minutes sitting on the edge of the circle, you are passed a balloon. You inhale the gas, and for thirty seconds your mind is up amongst the stars, staring back down at Earth.

It is an hour later and many people have gone home, like bathwater trickling down the plughole. Only the sediment remains. In the centre of the living room, Maria and her foreign friend dance in slow motion. Around the edges of the room are the unmoving shapes of a number of boys, their eyes tracing every movement of the girls.

You are not exempt from this, and as you watch them dance, you realise that tonight will not be your night. You turn to leave the room and almost bump into the Italian girl, Caterina. She moves towards you and soon you are kissing. Nothing will happen tonight with Maria and so you let Caterina lead you upstairs to your bedroom. Sleeping with a girl – any girl – will make you feel better. You begin to have sex, but your heart isn't in it. The fairy lights are putting you off. They hang mournfully above your window like a banner at a surprise birthday party that the birthday boy or girl has not turned up to.

"I'll be back in a minute," you tell Caterina.

You pull on your trousers and leave the room. Sean's younger brother is visiting you from his university and has been having a good time. He comes towards you up the stars, his palm against the wall to steady himself.

"Hey," you say. "There's a girl in my room, can you ask her to leave? Politely?"

"Sure," he says.

You feel a great affection for him at this point. Anyone willing to do the dirty work of someone they have only met once before is either a good judge of character, or a born risk-taker. Either one is good.

You hide downstairs. A few people are still mooching about. Mark went to bed long ago, after many free balloons and many pancakes. "Bastard", you think. Sean and your other flatmates are sitting around. Frankie is long gone. He got too drunk and stumbled off down the road, his girlfriend chasing after him. He will later tell you he was sick in front of a bar, causing the owners to call the police.

There is a commotion on the stairs and Sean's brother appears, Caterina before him, looking like she's in no hurry to drag you back upstairs. She gathers her coat and scarf and leaves, blowing a can't-be-arsed kiss in your direction, then laughs as the door closes behind her. You head back to the living room to find Maria. Now is your chance. She brushes past you, her coat in her arms. A few lazy shouts of "Bye" echo after her from the boys in the front room.

"Maria, stay a bit longer?" you ask her.

She seems not to hear you and within a minute she and her second friend are gone.

Now there is nothing to do. The people who have hung on this long are housemates and good friends. Amongst them is a boy no one invited, called Dan who's passed out on the sofa. Dan is friends with Mark, but Mark didn't invite him. Mark makes a point of never inviting anyone to your parties, presumably with the hope that a low turn-out will help advance his misery.

Someone has begun to draw on Dan's head with a marker pen. You're so tired that this does not amuse you. You trudge upstairs to bed. Crisps have been crushed into the carpet. Mark will not clean this up tomorrow. You crawl into bed. One of Caterina's socks is on your pillow for some reason, and you throw this off into a dark corner. Then you reach up to turn out the fairy lights.

In the morning you are woken by the door creaking open as someone bursts into your room. Dan is standing in the doorway, looking as though he has just overcome an obstacle course to get there. He stands wheezing for a moment or two in the doorway. You close your eyes and pretend he's not there.

"The rugby has started!" he says, gasping in stale bedroom air.

You have never once engaged Dan in a conversation on the topic of rugby. You do not care about rugby. This is one of Dan's ploys to showcase his supposed masculinity, because all men must like sports.

"Fuck off, Dan," you say.

You turn away from him and go back to sleep, Caterina's second sock is stuck to your face. Now is not the time for consciousness.

Bukowski's Pub

So Bukowski runs the pub around the corner
'94 was a lie, Hank tricked the coroner
The laureate left America for another life
Kicked the fame and left the wife
He's landed here, 'South Of No North'
A quiet life, occasional flutter on a horse
He's given up drinking, except for wine
Lost interest in writing but he's gonna read mine
I'm spending my time becoming a barfly
Drinking makes me sick, but I'm giving it a try
I'm there every day, and most of the night
Drinking whisky and soda (light)
It's costing a lot but surely it's worth it
I nod at Hank, "Better poor than the postal service"
I try to engage him on the films of Mickey Rourke
But Bukowski shuffles by, he's got no time to talk
"What about Matt Dillon?" I cry
The bar goes silent and conversation dies
The barmaid says, "No more for you, love"
A look on Hank's face, waiting for the kick off
I go home and spend all night at the machine gun
Re-writing Hank's tales from when he was young
I wake up early Saturday and head to the pub
12 o'clock, get peckish, call Hank over for some grub
Asked for a sandwich, 'Ham On Rye' with a wink
The barmaid pushes past him to the sink
I say, "Women!" with a shake of my head,
Bukowski serves someone else instead
The pub's crowded but I fight my way through
"Charles! Bukowski, Chinaski, I'm just like you!

I'm a writer as well! And I've had bad acne!
It's better now," I mumble, "The girls love me!"
Hank pulls me close and whispers, "Listen, bub,
You can't come in here, talking crazy in my pub"
"Hank," I say, "You don't have to pretend
It's me; you're talking to a friend!"
His hand finds my throat and squeezes a gulp
"If you don't get out, I'll beat you to a Pulp"
"Say no more," I say, as his eyes start to narrow
"Going incognito, like the old Red Sparrow?"
"Just leave before I give you a clout"
I climb up on a table and begin to shout
"'There's a bluebird in my heart that wants to…'"
Bukowski drags me down, kicks me to the door and says
"Get out"

The Torture Of A Young Heart

They had the cat trapped under a cardboard box and were poking it through the holes they'd made in the lid. The cat hissed and bared its teeth at them as it backed into a corner. Its black fur stood up in ragged strips and the patches of bare skin were crusted over like scales.

The boy with the mousy hair watched as Tony thrust his stick into the box, jabbing faster and faster, his eyes bright and mean. The girl stood back from the group, caught somewhere between laughter and guilt as she glanced along the path, worried someone might stumble upon them.

The mousey-haired boy stood by the box, his stick hanging limply beside him.

"Had enough?" Jimmy asked.

The boy laughed then tried to hold his smile in place. "Let's let it go. It's nearly dead. You can see its skin."

Jimmy stared at him, pushing his tongue from one side of his mouth to the other.

"Let's go to the tree," the boy said.

The girl smiled in relief. The boy tried to catch her eye as he smiled back.

Tony jabbed at the captive cat again.

"Leave it alone," Jimmy said. He walked over and kicked the box, sending it skittering across the concrete. The cat glanced about then darted away under the hedge.

Tony stared after the cat. He turned, grinned at the others, then snapped his stick over his knee and threw the two new shards at the mousy-haired boy.

"Catch!"

They walked along under the August sun – a waxy ball of heat in the sky – heading towards their tree. In one week they would be starting secondary school and the friendships they'd made over this last summer would quickly wash away like sandcastles on the beach. The tree had been theirs for the summer and from the top of its boughs they could see everything in their town, or so they imagined.

They'd tried to construct a tree house from bits of wood salvaged from the local skip, but the tree top had been too narrow and there was no way for them to balance the stolen planks. Once, the mousy-haired boy was halfway up the tree when a sheet of wood fell from where Tony was working above, slicing through the thin branches as it fell towards him. Only Jimmy, halfway between the two boys, was able to save him by pinching the board out of its free-fall.

The foursome walked along. The boy with the mousy hair slipped to the back of the group where the girl had been walking alone.

"That was horrible, wasn't it?"

The girl scratched her arm as Tony and Jimmy shoved one another ahead. "What was?"

"The cat," the boy said.

"I didn't mind." There was silence for a minute then she said, "But it was nice of you to let him go" and hurried away to catch up with the others.

When the boy climbed into the cool space beneath the firs, Tony, Jimmy and the girl were huddled together, whispering. Tony glanced up as the boy entered and the boy knew then that they were talking about him. He ignored their conversation and kicked at the pine cones resting on the floor of dead needles.

The trio broke their huddle. Tony helped the girl climb up onto a low branch. She started climbing and soon passed out of sight above them.

Jimmy came and put his arm around the mousy-haired boy. He leaned close to his ear and whispered, "Do you like Nicole?" He flicked his fringe towards where the girl had disappeared among the low branches.

"She's all right," the mousy-haired boy said.

"You like her. You should ask her out," Jimmy said.

Out of the corner of his eye, the boy saw Tony rub a dirty hand across his mouth.

"Ask her out," Jimmy nodded.

The boy cast about for an excuse. Tony held a hand to his mouth. He paced back and forth, kicking at fallen branches.

When Tony came back towards them, the boy knew he had to speak up. "She's already with you," he said, nodding at Tony and trying to smile as though he were in on the joke.

Tony looked at Jimmy and pursed his lips.

"Nicole is with Tony," the mousy-haired boy said, feeling hot now.

"Ask her out!" Jimmy said again. He turned and shouted up the tree for Nicole to come down.

She re-appeared, as though she had been waiting just out of sight, and sat on a branch just above their heads with her blue dress tucked under her knees.

"He's got something to ask you." Jimmy clapped the mousy-haired boy on the back.

"Ask her!" he whispered.

Tony was leaning against the tree, by Nicole's dangling feet.

The boy knew there was no way out of it. He glanced up at Nicole and wondered if she could see his burning cheeks. "I..." he began, "I was wondering if you'd go out with me, Nicole?" Then immediately, looking around at the other boys, "I know she's already with Tony!"

His voice cracked as he said it.

Jimmy snorted. Tony bent over and put his hands on his knees. Nicole stared down at them all without saying anything. The boy made an effort to laugh but the sound that came out did not sound like laughter, and it didn't sound like his voice, either. He waited for the laugher to die down, wishing he was anywhere else.

"Let's go to the field," he said.

There was no answer.

He spoke again, and found he had managed to find his

own voice. "Let's go to the field."

The laughter slowed and the two other boys glanced at each other, then shrugged.

"Let's go to the field," Jimmy said.

They laid their bikes on the dry and dusty dirt track and stepped into the field, stems of wheat snapping and bending as they forged their trails. The mousy-haired boy pushed ahead of the group, running his hands over the golden heads of wheat. He heard voices laughing behind him and he knew he had been foolish, but didn't know what else he could have done.

There was a sudden thundering of footsteps, then Tony barged into him from behind, sending him sprawling forward.

"Oops," Tony said, his eyes unblinking as he looked down at the boy on the ground.

The boy stood up, smiled, turned his back to Tony and carried on walking. His hand found the wheat stems again. He began snapping the heads off and letting them fall heavily to the ground. There were nearly two more weeks until school started. It would be OK.

The laughter grew behind him.

The boy decided he did not want to be there anymore. He walked back to the others.

"I've got to go home," he said.

"Just say if you want to go," Jimmy said, the smile fixed to his face.

"I've got to go," the boy repeated.

"Do you want to go?"

"I've got to go," the boy said finally, and he pushed past them and broke into a run as the tears broke over his cheeks.

He gathered up his bicycle and scrambled away down the dirt path, the bike shaking beneath him as laughter carried after him beneath the August sun.

After Exams

After Exams I will:

Read and write and fuck and fight,
Howl at the moon, sleep at first light,
Smoke and drink and laugh and joke,
Lay in, stay out, sing, commit sins,
Kiss and touch and eat too much,
Swim and smile and run for miles,
Stop to look, take a picture, read a book,
Sit and think as the sun sinks,
Find meaning in the stars, headlights of faraway cars,
Remember old friends you won't see again,
Cornfields with your grandfather, way back when,
How you cut your chin when you were ten,
James Bond, a bed-sheet den,
A broken ankle, birthday candles,
Snapped guitar strings, clipped wings,
Paper rounds, primordial morning sounds,
Mexico and letting go,
Flora De Caña from sugar cane,
Paris and London, trying again,
Ferries and planes, faces, no names,
India and scars and home too far,
Exams and results, hangovers and slumps,
The future in the past, a pirate flag above a mast,
Rock and roll and adventure for the soul,
Literature and art, history, false starts,
A beard and a house, two dogs and a mouse,
Cats in trees, children with bloody knees,
A place on the earth then a place within it,

Look for yourself from start to finish,
Through books and films, and pictures and songs,
Try to live your whole life, long.

Crack Addicts And The
Oaxaca Bicycle Race

I was on the second flight of the day (Monterrey-Mexico City-Oaxaca) when the woman leaned across and asked if we were athletes. I glanced at the guy next to me. I'd long since grown tired of having the same conversations with every white person I met, so the pair of us had spent the first hour of the flight in silence.

The guy was looking at me like I might have the answer to the woman's question. I knew I wasn't an athlete, that much was certain (I get tired playing *Mario Cart*) but the guy next to me was small and compact, a wiry sort of fellow with a shaved head that looked like it might somehow make him better at sport.

The woman was still dangling across the aisle, and was about to get nudged out of the way by the drinks trolley, when the guy answered.

"I'm not an athlete," he said, like it was a question he was asked every day.

"Me neither," I said, over the top of the drinks trolley.

The woman sat back in her seat. "Oh, I thought you were taking part in the race."

The small wiry guy and I exchanged glances. It was obvious neither of us knew the slightest thing about any race, but, looking around the plane at the obsessive healthy-looking people of all nationalities crammed into their seats, it was clear that something was indeed afoot.

I looked down at my skinny, bright red arms, then across to my new friend. It was clear this woman was trying to wind us up.

My friend leaned across me and shouted across the

aisle. "Why did you think we were athletes?"

The woman smiled and leaned out to speak to us again. She was Mexican, around thirty, dressed in a sharp suit. "It's the Oaxaca Bicycle Race this weekend. Isn't that why you're here?"

She introduced herself as Marie and handed across her card. "I'm with Coca-Cola," she explained. "Call me if you need anything."

My friend and I stared at the card. I told him my name and he said "I'm Chuck. Where are we going? Waxaca?" He glanced out the window, as though the clouds might have signposts.

I wasn't sure how he could have gotten on a plane without knowing where he'd be getting off again, but it appeared he had. I thought about offering to help him, but he spent the time until we landed hissing "Fuck, fuck, fuck!" under his breath, and I decided to stay out of it.

In the arrivals terminal I stood watching the baggage go round and round the carousel, until there was nothing left. I hoped my luggage was somehow receiving special treatment, but my hopes weren't high.

Across the lobby, Chuck was locked in a phone booth. I couldn't hear what he was saying, but his face was red and his fingers picked frantically at a poster stuck to the glass.

I walked to the information desk and told them my bag was still in Mexico City. Somehow, the woman behind the desk did not seem to understand my broken Spanish. Behind me, Chuck had found Maria, who seemed to be calming him down. The lobby was emptying and a black SUV was idling outside. Maria put her arm around Chuck and drew him towards the car. Here I was, luggage-less in a town I had never been to before, and the only people I even slightly knew were about to take off into the afternoon traffic. I abandoned the woman at the counter mid-sentence and dashed after Maria and the only other Gringo around.

Maria smiled when she saw me, and Chuck seemed relieved that he was no longer the only native English speaker around. I explained the situation and Maria went

84

across to the desk and began yelling at the woman in Spanish, telling her that she had better locate my bags. Muy rapido.

While Maria was thus engaged, Chuck filled me in on his situation, seeming to relax for the first time since I'd met him. "Man, I was heading to this rehab centre down in Puerto Angel. My mom packed me off, but somehow I've ended up here."

My immediate reaction was almost, "What drugs do you like, then?" then I changed my approach and told Chuck we'd get him there eventually.

Maria returned. Everything was taken care of, she said. They'd have the luggage sent to her hotel. She bundled us out of the airport and into the SUV. A huge Latino guy was waiting in the backseat. He pumped our hands and embraced Maria. Then the car took off and Maria introduced the big guy as Joel, a once-famous bicycle racer.

We ploughed through traffic, the air-conditioning making a nice change from the stuffy taxis I usually found myself in after arriving in a new town. Crates and crates of sports drinks were stuffed into the backseat and we had to balance on top of them. It turned out Maria was there to represent this drink (part of the Coca-Cola 'family') at the race, and she invited us to take as much as we wanted. Chuck and I gulped down some blue isotopes without making too much of a face.

A hotel appeared ahead. The car wound round and round, heading up a manicured path flanked by meticulously pruned bushes, then dropped us off next to a huge terracotta archway. Chuck and I glanced at each other again and did our best to refuse when Maria said she would get us a room on the sports drink's account.

"It's fine," I said. "I'll find a hostel, don't worry."

"No, no no," Maria said, waving her hands like my words were gnats she was brushing away.

"You say you are a pair of models, working for us, and I'll get you a room," she said, the upgrade from athletes feeling good.

Chuck and I stood waiting awkwardly while Maria argued with the hotel desk. It was obvious her technique was less successful than at the airport, and we would have to leave and try another hotel. Again, Chuck and I tried to refuse her hospitality, insisting we were used to hostels, but Maria was having none of it.

There was only one room – a twin – available at the next hotel and Maria booked all three of us in without mentioning the third person to the reception staff. Joel had found a room at the first hotel, and Maria had a meeting to attend so she gave Chuck her mobile number and said we should call her later, insisting as she left that we should eat and drink whatever we want and charge it to her. Chuck and I walked to the room, past men in Lycra shorts, stretching and adjusting things on their bicycles. By this point, it seemed a good idea to just go with the flow.

The room was large, the sun shone through the window and the bed sheets were white. I took a shower and Chuck leant me a clean t-shirt. Then, sitting on the balcony, I was about to take a beer from the minibar until I remembered Chuck's addiction and suggested we look around instead.

The hotel restaurant put on a buffet for the race competitors and Chuck and I made sure we were the first people there. We sat in the empty restaurant and I loaded up on pulled pork and chicken legs – a feast after two months of cheap tacos. Chuck sat nervously, repeating that we'd get in trouble.

As the restaurant filled up, Chuck opened up about how he'd got here. He told me he'd worked in the U.S. Navy, out in the Gulf, but it hadn't worked out for him, and eventually he was dishonourably discharged and had spent the past six months smoking crack on his bathroom floor. Finally, his 'mom' had had enough and shipped him out to a rehab centre down on the southern coast of Mexico, which is when our paths had crossed.

Just as we were finishing our plates, Chuck's phone rang. It was Maria, inviting us out for drinks. She was in a bar with the famous cyclist Dirk Strongman, and if we hurried, we might meet him. I knew nothing of Dirk back then (he was still respectable at this time), other than that he was a fan of yellow wristbands, but it seemed like the right thing to do to round out this strange day, so I persuaded Chuck to come along, promising him we could leave the bar any time he wanted to.

The bar was swanky and everyone wore suits and flashed their new watches as they called the waiters across for more champagne or tequila. Chuck glanced around nervously as we found seats beside Maria. Joel was sitting at our table with another, equally-large Italian, who had also been a champion racer in his time. Maria ordered us drinks and Chuck stared at his for half an hour, before pushing it in front of me.

"There's Dirk," Maria whispered. And there he was, a few tables away with his back to us.

Maria brought him across and Joel and the Italian pumped his hand enthusiastically like they were old friends. We stood in a line for a photo and I asked Dirk to sign my (Chuck's) white t-shirt. (I later sold this t-shirt for £15 on eBay. In hindsight I should have kept it until after he'd been revealed as a dirty cheat).

Chuck and I left soon after, and by the time we got back to the hotel, I could tell he was feeling a little worse for wear. There were only two beds in the room and we took one each. Maria had invited us to share her room, and offered to pay for everything, so we thought we'd see whether she'd mind sharing a bed with one of us. It turned out that she did. The door opened in the night and Maria stood silhouetted in the doorway, giggling as she grasped the hand of a large man. Then the door shut and their sounds scattered away down the corridor.

The next day was the day of the bicycle race and Maria had managed to secure us V.I.P passes. We stood in a sort of marquee on scaffolding, watching the racers line up below. Dirk appeared to start the race, then, as he set the cyclists off, he walked back up the track against them, a self-assured salmon swimming against the stream of wheels glinting in the sun. Everyone in the V.I.P booth shook their heads and began muttering, but I didn't care about cycling, or Dirk Strongman, and was only concerned with the canapés.

The afternoon passed slowly as the cyclists trailed tirelessly past. Maria pointed out various people: the Mayor of Oaxaca; the head of Mexico's biggest telecoms company; a Mexican soap star. A little later, as Chuck and I were working up the nerve to ask for a photo with the models from the telecoms company, Maria told us she had to pop out, but would be right back. Ten minutes later, Chuck claimed he had to call his 'mom'. He left, sniffing and rubbing the back of his hand against his cheek and I found myself alone among the Oaxacan elite.

I decided to approach the models. A photograph was taken, then immediately afterwards, a short, burly official took me under the arm and bundled me out of the V.I.P area. All my connections to that world had left me, and my time among the important people was up.

I spent the rest of the day wandering around, looking for Chuck, but I never found him. I was stopped now and then by locals asking for pictures with me, their children clinging to my legs. After a while, I took off the V.I.P lanyard and threw it away.

I went back to the hotel, found my luggage had arrived, and checked out of the room. I dug out my guidebook and found a hostel, where I met new people and new things happened. I never saw Chuck again, and I only remembered he existed once Dirk Strongman was exposed as a cheat.

Dirk was able to manipulate his drug abuse and earned millions upon millions of dollars, lying to others all the while. Chuck, on the other hand, ended up becoming abused by the drugs, losing his job, and being packed off to another country by his mother. I think about Chuck sometimes and wonder whether he ever made it to that rehab centre by the coast, or if he simply melted away into the ciudades of southern Mexico. I suppose I'll never know.

Resolution

You don't want to hit the guy. You don't have anything against Australians and it *is* New Year's Eve, after all. Plus, you haven't seen him do anything wrong. But, when you're in Paris with a group of prima donna cabaret dancers, you'd better be doing something to earn your place.

"Haaaarry. That guy just touched me...there."

What are you doing there, lost in some club in the depths of Paris? A short and narrow club that could fit thirty people at most, like a VIP-only freight container smuggling everyone into the New Year. It isn't the first club of the night. It had started out well. Champagne and aperitifs backstage at the Moulin Rouge. That was the first time you'd asked yourself what you were doing.

More champagne. Shrieks. Tequila in the dressing rooms and then a walking fashion show overflowing into the streets. Black, gold, red, blue dresses, high heels, designer bags, the taste of champagne and the freedom of the Parisian night. Then you're walking through the cold night air and it doesn't matter that she's slightly ahead and you imagine this is a normal night for her, that you're witnessing what she does for the 350 days of the year you aren't there, when you're back in England, drinking with medical students, drama-drop outs and wannabe-Hemingways.

You make your way to the first club, the girls' heels clicking on the night-time pavements, cries from all corners of Europe welcoming the early hours of the virgin year. You arrive at a grand old ballroom that seems to be empty but are greeted by a fruity Frenchman wearing an expensive suit and haircut. He sets about the group, kissing the dancers like they went back thirty years. None of the girls have seen thirty years and the host has paralysed his face to pretend he hasn't either.

And then it's free champagne under the golden chandeliers and deep red of the walls and the painted angels on the ceiling. A half-empty dance floor and her getting annoyed because the free champagne only stretched to one glass each and this isn't enough for you to dance, but you're out with twenty dancers who need no encouragement so your moves look amateur to say the least and you're starting to get pissed off with her jokes about your lack of coordination.

You're left alone with some of her friends and are light-heartedly hit on by a Frenchman. You pretend you are the boyfriend of one of the other dancers (another Australian) and you all leave the club, some of the group fracturing off to find their own way into the earliest hours of the New Year on this wildest of nights.

"Where now?"

And she tells you, "Ivan – he's a really good friend of mine – he's organised for us to go to another club. He's going to drive us."

A really good friend. But it turns out it isn't like that. Ivan is Nadia's fiancée, whoever Nadia is. He drives a few of you to the freight container then disappears into Paris to pick up the rest of the troupe. Soon everyone is reunited and half the girls file into the bathroom to do lines with Ivan before he dashes out again to ferry more fellow revellers.

And now there are no free drinks and you start to sober up. Some fat cats in suits are pouring the girls free vodkas. She asks if you want one. She has to pass you it in private because the men only want to give the girls drinks and you have to stand there and watch them all flirt just to get a drink and you're beginning to think you aren't feeling it anymore.

And then suddenly, some Australian who'd had too many, snakes his hand across her and you're being called upon to defend her honour in front of all of her drunken friends. Now supposedly your drunken friends.

You remember years ago when you used to live back in that small English town and she had always said, "I hate violence."

You remember the time when you pushed a guy for dancing with her and she ran off crying and you felt compelled to apologise. But Paris has made her want you to kill this guy. She's a V.I.P. and punishment is her right. You're angrier at yourself for getting into this situation than the Australian, but you push him and ask him what the fuck he thinks he's doing.

Then *his* girlfriend shrieks and your girl takes her arm and explains to her slowly and clearly that her boyfriend is the lowest type of scum and that you can't go around acting like that because it's just disrespectful and if it were her boyfriend she'd be sickened and why did she want to be with a man like that?

The girls' attention is back on you. You tell the guy that if he does it again you're going to break his fucking nose. This seems to be what your girl wants and so you push him and he's so drunk so he stumbles over a table and sends all the drinks crashing down to the floor with him.

Now the rest of the Australians are standing up and you know it's game over and you're in the process of trying to man up to them when the bouncers come over, shouting in French. It's definitely game over, except it isn't because now she's speaking to the bouncer. You don't understand what she's saying but she flashes the V.I.P wristband and soon everything's OK and the Australian guy sits down with his mates and his girlfriend (who by now is crying her eyes out).

Now you're back in your little group and the other girls are back from doing coke or talking to the guys for the free vodka and they're asking what happened. She tells them, "That idiot tried to touch me up so Harry pushed him over."

But it's matter-of-fact. There's no thanks or "You're my hero" in her voice, just disinterestedness, as though she's telling someone what she had for dinner.

91

Then, although things have calmed down, it's time to leave because Cocaine Ivan has another party organised for the group. You ask who made him the official party planner but everyone ignores you and soon you're pushed into the back seat of Ivan's car while his Russian fiancée screams at him as city lights slip past the windows.

Then you're in another club on the Champs-Élysées and it doesn't get much more glamorous than this. Oh, what a fantastic new year. You're in the club; V.I.P again. But there's a problem. They expect your group to *pay* to use the cloakroom.

So moody Nadia the Russian leads you through the club and marches up to the same eccentric Frenchman who owned the first club. There are more hugs and endless kisses – on both sets of cheeks – and then you're at your own private cloakroom and *of course* you don't have to pay. Even you, the quiet Brit following along with your manners and your pleases and thank yous, only here because of her, no one else questioning your presence or not noticing and very likely not caring.

And then you're back where you belong, back in V.I.P with your complimentary champagne. This time, though, there's enough for you to finally start feeling like it's New Year's Eve. The music is flowing and the drinks are ringing in your ears. You realise you're twenty-years-old and in Paris with a group of beautiful cabaret dancers and again you wonder what the hell you're doing there.

Everyone's feeling ever so happy now that you're settled in this new club. Ivan has left and Nadia seems calmer. You need to get a picture of yourself surrounded by all these girls (to show off to the medical students, the drama drop-outs and the wannabe-Hemingways) so the girls crowd around you and do their best smile. Practised to perfection backstage with footballers and rock stars. She's sitting on her own looking spaced out but happy. She always was a lightweight. She's started giving you her champagne, which is fine by you.

The champagne has made you one of the gang and you

talk to a beautiful Austrian redhead while your girl rests in the corner. She's looking distant but happy and keeps glancing over as the Australian plays with her hair. Part of you wants to show her that you could get girls like this if you wanted to. She left you to come here, to this country, and now you're a free man. While she's out there with her friends in Paris being a V.I.P, you're doing just as well back home with your own friends. But this is only ten percent of what you're feeling. You're not angry any more. Everything is fun now.

Then the night slowly winds down as the sun creeps over the horizon, a new light on the old streets. The festivities splutter and die and you get into a taxi. More hugs and kisses with her friends. Almost your friends too, by now; the hugs and kisses almost genuinely affectionate.

Then you're away, just the two of you in the back of the taxi and it feels like it's the first time you've been together all night. All year. She smiles and asks if you've had a good time. Then she tells you she was a little bit jealous when you were talking with her friends. She smiles as if she's being silly and you want to pull her towards you and tell her not to worry but you can't because you aren't those people to each other anymore. She smiles again and then you're back at her flat.

You walk in for the first time that year. The one-room studio is still a mess from before you went out earlier that night and smells of the special dinner you ate still linger. It was good then, your home-cooked meal and homemade cocktails and how you sweated through midnight. The flat was a cocoon from the outside world and your celebrations with just the two of you felt more real than the plastic showbiz evening that came afterwards. But even now it's clear you're both acting. Pretending nothing had happened over the last two years, all the while knowing that the two of you together in Paris in any form was only fleeting. Her life there is real, and for her alone. And perhaps she has forgotten what had been real to her back home, before Paris became her new reality and you found a new reality of your own.

Soon after you leave Paris in the glow of the January sun, wondering where next New Year's Eve will find you and knowing you'll never come back or see her again.

A Bike Ride

The film ended and darkness illuminated the room
Some rose to leave and some stayed, held in their seats by a
residue of the screen
He was among those who rose and collected their coats
He made his way down the wooden staircase and out
into the night, past old men who stood,
their cigarette smoke like frost in the night

The combination lock had changed during the film
but cold fingers found it and freed the bike and then he was
away
the roads were uneven and people, like deer,
staggered along between fisherman's bars
He ducked between them, past the church,
past closed shops, lit bright in the night

He stopped on a bend and a car passed, nothing more than a
collection of lights
Onwards was darkness and the twisting street which he rode
like a wave,
the Atlantic on both sides and in the air the smell of salt
Midnight, also, in the air, and spectres from the leftover
pumpkins that guarded gardens
that he passed with arms wide like the wings of a bird
Above, more stars than could exist but the same
constellation that stood over his backyard at home

The movie was in his mind and the salt air in his lungs
The frost was on his cheeks but the darkness did not matter
as the bicycle bumped and rocketed its way onwards

Trees and dark wooden houses bordered him and in-
between, glimpses of the bay
But his eyes were upwards still on the brilliance of the stars
and he did not see the car as it came over the hill

The Woman Of My Dreams

Dear Diary,

Like most things beyond our grasp, she came to me in a dream. I am, however, inclined to question whether it was a dream at all, so vivid were its colours and so real the emotions which it stirred within me. I write this now as I take my breakfast in the den, my wife hovering nearby, asking and asking me whether I shall be late for work.

At present she's advising me on the Tube and how busy it will be – as if she's ever taken the Tube anywhere in her life. There is a strange satisfaction, knowing what happened in my dream. It is almost like another life, a secret affair. I'm trying now to hide the warm feeling in my stomach and stop it spreading to my face. Happiness is not permitted by my wife, at least, not my own happiness. It's a direct affront to her own misery, or faux misery, as is realistically the case.

Anyway, never mind my wife. I've wasted enough time writing about her. Now I shall lay down the contents of my dream so that if it is to be the only time I encounter her, I will always have this record. To begin with, we (and I'm not sure who 'we' were, except myself and another man) were flying in some sort of bomber plane over Europe. The historical setting was decidedly WW2, as I was able to deduce from our outfits. We were on a mission, about to release our cargo over the enemy below.

Suddenly, the other man, twirling his moustaches, informed me that the target had changed. We were now about to land at home, where our assumed allies were waiting to ambush us as soon as we stepped off the plane.

Naturally, this would not do. I was sent scurrying into

the bowels of the plane to find suitable weaponry, which I was able to do in the form of a collection of Thompson submachine guns, Sten guns and assorted pistols.

Here the dream became even more peculiar. I brought the weapons back into the large cockpit and was instructed to dump them on some sort of 'dashboard' as though the plane was in fact a car. We were swooping in low over our betrayers now and through large windows we could see our target. As the engines roared in our ears the moustachioed man shouted, "Give them hell!" and started shooting through the window with a Sten gun.

As the glass whirled around us I reached for my own weapon, only to find that all of the guns had turned into toys and I was helpless to do anything but watch as the plane crashed into the ground.

Now, all of this was of no real consequence, and probably resulted from the film I saw just before bed. The real excitement came when I seemed to wake up after the plane crash. I found myself in a bed I had not slept in for years, some relic of a forgotten student house. My body too was younger, but I was not sure how young, certainly not older than twenty.

I lay for a moment, unsure what I was doing or where I was, when a shape appeared beside me in the bed. It was the loveliest shape I've ever seen, with long, narrow legs leading forever upwards to the smallest of black cocktail dresses. Long, narrow arms like the branches of a willow stretched from the dress and the face of an angel smiled at me from beneath golden hair. It was love at first sight.

I was unable to speak. Something told me she was some figure of authority, and so I waited for her to break the silence, which she did with a smile.

"Ah, you are awake."

The accent was of some Eastern-European origin. Soviet Union, if we're staying with the war theme. She was lovely. Her voice was lovely and if I had been awake I would have been sure I was dreaming.

I said something then, but was unable to hear my voice.

The girl smiled. It was the sort of smile that sets your heart on fire. I could feel my body regenerating already.

"What's your name?" I asked.

"But you already know," she answered in her perfect voice, causing my heart to fall into my stomach and fireworks to explode in my mind.

The girl rose to leave, smoothing the dress around her thighs.

"Don't," I said.

She smiled. "I'll see you soon, you know that."

I pulled her down beside me but she resisted my attempts to bring her closer to me.

"A kiss before you leave?" I asked.

She shook her head as if full of mischief. Her hand slipped beneath the sheets and a finger ran along my testicles and then she jumped up and was gone.

As you can imagine, when I woke beside my wife it was with great disappointment. I had a feeling like a great wave of despair had suddenly washed me below the surface, and I became aware for the first time in my life that I had been treading water the whole time and was yet to start swimming.

Now, as the children scream and my wife scolds them, I shall finish this entry and head for the safety of the Tube tunnels.

Dear Diary,

Awoke in a foul mood today. Awful day at work yesterday, Joseph has become section manager. Of all the outrageous nonsense... Came home to the wife telling me we need a new car, and with what money? Sleep was no release. No sign of my Eastern beauty, instead I dreamed of cars and disciplinaries and have woken up feeling worse than ever.

Dear Diary,

She returns! The literal woman of my dreams. I can still smell her. She smells of cake. Pink cake with icing and *ribbons and all that sort of thing. I sit here writing and breathe her in deeply. She has travelled from my dreams to sit beside me at breakfast and every word my wife says falls on deaf ears.*

I awoke last night in a different bed again; this time in a garden of pink roses with my angel there in a glowing white dress, leading me through the foliage. We climbed a grassy hill and at the top saw the sea stretching for miles in the moonlight, silver ripples on the water. My angel told me her name and where she came from and we talked for an eternity. I remember nothing of what we said but at the same time I'm certain that I know everything there is to know about her, and she about me. Without even speaking we had forged a connection a thousand times more powerful than all the words ever exchanged between myself and my wife.

Finally, after hours of talking, the dreamlike apparition slid her dress over her shoulders and revealed beneath...It's too much to write down. I'm afraid that I cannot capture the pure ecstasy fully enough. I am afraid I shall lose details and damage the memory in my fumbled attempt at writing,, so for now the event remains (constantly) within my mind.

Dear Diary,

The love of my life evades me! For a whole week now I have not dreamt of her. I have even begun to follow the same routine each night before I go to sleep. I eat the same meal, do the same exercises, even re-watch the same war film that I viewed on that first night. My wife thinks I am going insane. Of course I have not told her the reason for this routine, this religious preparation for the nightly raptures that increasingly evade me.

These night-time excursions have become more real to me than my day life. 'Day life' is what I call it now. This endless job and this nagging wife whose only achievement in life has been to grow into a cliché now feel more like a dream to me. My children – spoilt, fat little brats whom I hardly know. I spend my days working for them, and for nothing. No gratitude, not from them nor my bosses. I'm continually overlooked, undervalued and underused. It is as though I exist as a pillar to prop up the lives of those around me. They rest atop me like smug busts without any concept of how the plinth supports them beneath.

Dear Diary,

Tonight it happened! I'm writing this by candlelight in the bathroom, for fear of discovery… Not thirty minutes ago, my angel appeared to me again, out of the darkness.

She took my head in her hands and she said, "Don't worry my dear…don't worry. Soon we can be together always."

She told me how to do it and I don't know why I haven't thought of it before. I can barely contain my excitement.

Diary,

I write this from the breakfast table. I have not slept! All night I lay awake in bed beside my wife, thinking how much I hate that woman. My angel appeared beside me when I closed my eyes and I wrapped my arm around her neck. Tonight we shall be together forever and there will be nothing to stop me from finally achieving happiness.

Diary,

I could barely contain myself at work. All day long I had a barely suppressible smile on my lips, one that was the envy of all my co-workers. All day long I caught them glancing at me as though wondering what was going on in my mind. As if they were baffled that someone should be happy! Well, happy I am. I even helped an old lady on to the Tube and nothing my wife had said has been able to dint my elation.

There was a bit of trouble on the way home, I had to stop by four different pharmacies to get the required amount. I thought briefly about leaving a note, but then, it's not really a suicide if your life is about to begin, is it? A note would be good though, I could comment on the irony of having to sleep to be fully awake. It would probably be lost on my wife.

No, no note.

It doesn't feel how I had envisioned it would. I feel a bit lightheaded, woozy. Things are funny that wouldn't normally be. I'm watching the war film again. There are two packets left. I'll get through them before she gets back with the children. Then I think I'll go up to bed and have a nice lie down. Yes, that'll be nice.

***

She didn't see the diary when she came in, somehow he had knocked it under the bed and there it remained. What she did see were the empty packets of sleeping tablets on the kitchen counter and the empty bottle of scotch beside them.

"Wait outside," she told the children and when they protested she poked the nearest one in the forehead. "Do as I say."

She walked into the dark house. It didn't seem right to turn the lights on. What had that bastard done now? That selfish, selfish bastard. How were they going to pay the mortgage now, with him gone? The children would have to move school, they couldn't afford that now. Her brother would have to help them out again.

She found him in the bedroom, sprawled across the bed like a starfish. Selfish bastard. She kicked him in the stomach and his body wobbled. A faint murmur escaped his lips and she knew he was still there.

***

He came round with a smile, muttering under his breath, she noted in disgust. She'd had to sit there for two days while he slept. All the engagements she'd missed…

Then he came to, fully awake. He looked startled, glancing from one side to another, not recognising the hospital room.

"I hope you're ashamed of yourself," she said.

He seemed too preoccupied to notice her. She poked him in the ribs and he winced with pain.

He had failed. There was no way out. "Yes dear, I'm so sorry. I don't know what I was thinking. Are the children here?"

"Yes," she said.

Perhaps after all…

"They've been worried sick, waiting for days. Oh, the things we've had to re-arrange because of you. The trouble you've caused…"

"They can't see me like this, the children," he said, sitting up and pulling the bedclothes to his chest. "Will you give me a minute alone, to get ready for them?"

"Yes, you'd better sort yourself out," she said, narrowing her eyes.

"I think I'll have a shave," he said, scratching his chin. "Could you pass me my razor, dear?"

She threw across the wash bag she'd hastily packed for him while they waited for the ambulance. "Find it yourself."

She stormed out of the room.

"See you later then, dear," he said to himself. Then, "See you soon, my love."

A Loss Of Innocence

The ball caught the blonde boy's forehead. It was no accident and he flicked his head slightly to the left and the ball flew like a bird and hit the goalkeeper's face like an egg. The keeper dropped to his knees, a small amount of blood dripping from his nose on to the grass and the dirty gloves he held to his face. The blonde boy ran over to where the ball waited. A tall boy with black hair dressed in a red jersey ran up beside him but the blonde boy pulled the ball away and struck it with his laces. The ball skimmed past the goalkeeper's ear, causing him to duck as the ball spun off across the field behind him.

Later, the blonde boy staggered under the weight of a pile of tattered orange cones, his feet slipping in the mud.

"Careful there!" the teacher said as he ran past in his grey tracksuit, kicking up clods of earth behind him. He'd only gone a few metres when he turned and called back over his shoulder. "You played really well tonight! Well done."

The boy smiled and hurried after him. A moment later he slipped on the mud and dropped the cones.

Most of the boys had gone home by now, their mothers had other places to be and they waited impatiently by their cars outside the school. One by one the boys had trickled out, laughing and shouting, alive with the excitement of football and running through the school corridors hours after the school day had ended.

"That was fucking great, mate," the tall boy with black hair said in the changing rooms as he threw his red jersey into his bag and pulled his school shirt over his sweat streaked body.

"Just doing what I do," the blonde boy said.

They laughed together then the other boy picked up his bag and his mud-caked shoes and headed for the door.

"My mum's waiting outside, she goes fucking nuts if I'm late. See you tomorrow."

"Yeah, see you tomorrow."

The blonde boy was alone now as he pulled his t-shirt over his head and threw it on the floor where it landed with a wet slap. He was muscular for his age but his arms remained thin, no matter how many press ups he tried to do. He sat down and kicked off his football boots, then pulled off his long socks like snake skins. The tiled floor was cool beneath his feet and he wasted a moment, reading the graffiti on the wall and trying to work out how much the coins under the opposite bench added up to.

He stood up and padded across the changing room, his feet sticking on the wet floor. He knelt in his shorts and reached under the bench, his nails scraping up mud and clumps of hair and old pens and cigarette butts. He ran his hand over the grime again and felt the coins and slid them out towards him.

When he raised his head to count the money he fell back in surprise. The teacher was standing over him, his grey tracksuit trousers at the boy's eye level.

"Oh, you're still here?" the teacher said, extending a hand to help the boy up.

The nails were dirty, the boy noticed as he was pulled to his feet.

"Thanks… I was, I saw some money under the bench." He held out the grubby mess of coins for inspection.

The teacher bent forward to look, bringing his face close to the boy's. "That's not a lot of money," he said.

He looked up quickly and smiled as he met the boy's eyes.

"Look, you've done really well today, why don't you take this?" he asked.

The boy watched his hand move about in inside his tracksuit pocket, then re-emerge with a folded five pound note.

"I can't," the boy said.

"Of course you can."

The teacher tapped him on the arm. 'You've got some big shoulders there.'

The boy said nothing but tried to glance at his shoulders out of the corner of his eyes.

"Your mum doesn't come to pick you up does she?' the teacher said and the boy felt a hot flush of embarrassment.

"No."

"What was that?" the teacher asked. He leaned in close again and the boy could see how his brown stubble was flecked with grey.

"No, she doesn't pick me up… she works," the boy said, staring at his bare feet in case there was a better answer there. His toes seemed child-like to him and he felt awkward now, half-dressed and halfway between a child and a man.

"Well," the teacher said, pressing the five pound note into the boy's hands. "Take this, and get a bus home. You did well today."

The boy felt the crumpled paper in his hand. "Thanks."

"I think you could be captain of the under-fourteens," the teacher said and the boy forgot the money as his eyes darted up to meet his teacher's.

"Really?"

"Yes."

The teacher sat down on the bench and gently pulled the boy down beside him. The boy felt his teacher's thigh against his. He edged away slightly and the teacher slid along to fill the gap absentmindedly.

"You're a great footballer. You look great out on the pitch," he said. His fingers brushed the boy's knee, seemingly of their own accord.

"I have to go," the boy said, standing up.

"What time's your bus?" the teacher asked, looking up slowly from the bench

"What?"

"I just gave you money for a bus, what time does it come?"

"Oh. I'm not sure. Soon, though."

"Soon," the teacher repeated as the boy began to pull his backpack on.

"Hey," the teacher laughed. "You can't go out there like that, you're half naked!"

The boy realised with embarrassment that he was still wearing only his shorts and he put down his bag down and began to rummage through it for his clothes.

"Aren't you going to have a shower?" the teacher asked, standing up.

"No, I'll have one at home."

"Your mum won't be too happy if you get all your school clothes stinking of sweat, will she?"

"She's never too happy about anything," the boy answered before he could stop himself.

Silence fell for a few moments and then the teacher said softly, "There's no reason to make her more angry, then, is there?"

The boy continued through the motions of rummaging through his bag.

"You should have a shower. You can't go home all muddy."

The boy felt something suddenly touch his shoulder. Without thinking he shuddered and ducked away.

"Sorry. It's only me," the teacher said, his hand half outstretched. "It's only me. Get in the shower and have a wash, then you'll just have enough time to get the bus," he said with a smile.

"I'm all right," the boy said.

The teacher started to unzip his jacket. "I'll tell you what, I need a shower too, so we can share one to save time, eh?"

The teacher continued undressing and slid his t-shirt over his head. Out of the corner of his eye the boy saw his chest, sprouting with hairs, thick like the wires that grew from his grandmother's moles. The boy felt sick but didn't

107

know what to do and then, suddenly, the teacher was standing naked beside him and he couldn't help but see it, hanging heavily.

"Let's get clean, then!" the teacher said. "Come on, get those shorts off!"

He reached out a hand to the boy's waistband but the boy stepped back and slowly lowered the shorts and his underwear himself, his own thing like some stubby mushroom.

The teacher said nothing for a moment, then, "Come on then, let's get you cleaned up." He took the boy by the hand and led him into the showers, the stale smell of sweat following them.

***

They had won the tournament and his team lifted him above their shoulders and carried him as their champion. He held the bronze cup aloft, like the head of a defeated enemy. The crowd of teenagers roared and his teammates cheered and threw their fists in the air then turned to jeer the losing team who slinked away to their changing room, their chins resting on their chests.

The champions marched into the foreign dressing rooms, studs clacking on the tiled floor like spears against shields. They undressed among laughter and jokes and then the tall boy with black hair said, "To ——!" and the teammates turned to the boy with the blonde hair and cheered once more.

The boy blushed, then recovered and bowed. "Thanks for the help, lads. We fucking killed them!"

The boys roared.

The sports teacher came into the room, grinning widely, shaking hands as he passed.

The blond boy looked away.

"Right, boys! Time to get clean, into the shower, you sweaty bastards!"

The boy slid in among the crowd as they surged towards

the cubicles. In the middle of these wet bodies he was safe.

The celebrations had continued on the coach home, but the blonde boy had fallen quiet, replying it was hard work being a champion whenever anyone asked him what was wrong.

When they arrived back outside the school the boy slipped off the bus, unnoticed except for the teacher who came down the steps towards him. The teacher opened his mouth as though he were about to say something, but the boy turned and walked quickly away. All the way home he could feel something wet and heavy against his back.

When he got in, his old man was sitting with the lights off, the room lit by the television.

"Where's mum?" the boy asked.

"Question of the century," the old man said, his back to the boy.

The boy went into the kitchen and opened the fridge. All there was to eat was half a loaf of bread and some old cheese. He could go out and buy some food. There was still the five pound note, tucked under his bed, untouched since the night he had come home under cover of darkness and hidden it there. The boy did not want to touch it. No matter how hungry he was, he had to keep it hidden away and then maybe the things it reminded him of would never have happened.

Bread and cheese would have to do. He scraped the mould away as best he could and made himself a sandwich then walked back into the lounge. He sat down beside his dad and dropped his sports bag heavily on the carpet. The man didn't get the hint, his eyes stuck on the television.

The boy watched along with him in silence for a few minutes. His father was watching a war film. Parts of jungles exploded and little Asian men with strange hats ran, on fire, from out of the tree line. The boy pictured his teacher on fire, writhing about on the floor in agony. He clenched his fists until his hands were numb. He felt that if he kept this feeling hidden inside of him, he would drown beneath its weight. His mind twisted and struggled against itself, undecided about whether he should say something to his father. He knew it hadn't been his fault, but his old man might not be so understanding. He felt that the words would come tumbling out now, whether he wanted them to or not. He decided he had to take control of these words so that at least he could guide them into his father's ears in a way that would do as little damage as possible.

"Dad…" he began, his tongue feeling dead in his mouth.

"What?" the old man answered as an American soldier emptied his M16 into a woman and her baby.

"Erm…" the boy said, his stomach twisting itself round and round.

"What?" the old man said again, his anger rising in his voice.

"We…we won the tournament today."

"Hmm," the old man said.

The boy said nothing more. He gathered up his bag and his sandwich and went up to his room. Once there he took the five pound note out from under his bed and opened the bedroom window. He stood for a minute staring at the face on the note, then he opened a drawer and took out his box of matches. He struck one and held the flame against the money. The paper was quickly eaten up as a black line spread across its surface, driven by flames.

The boy held the note as long as he could, hardly noticing the heat burning his fingers, then he let the scraps fly out into the air like the flaming wreck of a paper plane. He watched until the flames were pinched out by the night and the note was no more.

***

The next day the boy arrived late to school. As he walked into his first classroom the other children stood up and began to cheer. He nodded his gratitude, held his hands up before them for silence, then motioned for them to sit down. When the history teacher told him to stop causing a commotion, he glared at her until she was quiet, made his way slowly to his seat, then nodded at her to begin.

The Sweetest Meat

Hugo's legs shook as he thundered downhill. He was breathing heavily and when the road flattened out again he had to take a succession of deep breaths to return his air intake to normal.

The boughs of the trees arched over him, blocking out the remains of the purple evening light. Mosquitoes swarmed beside the stream and Hugo spat out flies as he ran, shivering as he imagined them becoming caught in his hair.

The path levelled out and Hugo's oversized running shoes pounded the gravel beneath his feet, the rhythmic crunch slipping into sync with his breathing. He had been running for an hour. This was his fourth time around the circuit, but today he'd needed to shake something out of his system. Today had been the final day of term before the summer holidays and, as expected, his pupils had gone insane. Before he had left the school grounds, Hugo had been covered in a lifetime's worth of shaving foam and had an egg smashed over his head. He hadn't seen the culprit because the force of the egg had knocked off his glasses, shattering them under the feet of kids eager to start their summer.

Hugo had a strong idea who was responsible, though. There was only one person it could have been. 'Little George Pearson'. Well, not really 'little'. More like 'Fat George Pearson'.

Hugo had never encountered a viler or more disgusting boy. Week after week George would disrupt Hugo's lessons, standing up on his desk and shouting and swearing, once even whipping his penis out and slapping it from side to side. Everyone had been amused. No matter how much Hugo shouted at him and sent him out of the room, the rest of the children treated George like a hero and Hugo was certain it had been George who had egged and floured him at the school gates. He also had a deep suspicion that it had been George (or George and his cronies) who had scratched his car with a key a month earlier.

The thought of the little bastard made Hugo run faster still. The trees shot past him and the stream bubbled steadily beside him. Sweat poured from his forehead and stung his eyes. Hugo had become accustomed to the sweat by now and wiped it away automatically. Thoughts of George and the other little fuckers left his mind. It was summer now and he wouldn't have to see any of them for six weeks. Maybe he would even go on holiday. If he could persuade anyone to go with him.

He thought suddenly of his last girlfriend. It had been over three years ago. He was thirty-four now and his mother constantly asked him when he'd be getting married. Well, she'd have to wait. The perfect girl was just around the corner, he was sure. They'd asked him about it today. His sex life.

"Sir, are you a virgin?"

In the middle of the chemistry lesson. He hadn't meant to go red in the face but he didn't know how else to react. His complexion had only encouraged them and in the end there had been nothing he could do to control them. He couldn't very well send the whole class out to the headmaster.

Hugo jogged onwards. A lot could happen in six weeks. He had little to do with no obligations. Maybe he'd find a girl. He was going to the gym tomorrow and now, with six weeks of freedom, he could build the perfect body. Or he hoped he would be able to. For four months now he had tried one protein shake after another, different protein-rich, high calorie diets and different workout routines, all in vain attempts to build muscle. Anything to stop the kids at school from calling him 'The Beanstalk' (often to his face).

Raw eggs for breakfast hadn't worked. Six meals a day of chicken breasts and broccoli hadn't helped. Steak and nuts for every meal hadn't made a difference. He'd got up in the middle of the night to eat, spent all Saturday snacking and tried eating a whole chicken a day, but still Hugo could not put on weight. He'd eaten ostrich and kangaroo and tuna and shark and venison and rabbit but none of it had helped. There was almost nothing he hadn't tried eating in his quest to bulk up.

But, as he thundered along, Hugo knew he must keep trying. 'The Beanstalk' had to die.

Another mile and Hugo began to tire and slow his pace. That fat little bastard George had no trouble putting weight on. Jesus. Hugo'd seen him at lunchtime, shovelling down mouthful after mouthful of deep-fried crap. Hugo shook his head. He had to forget about George if he was to relax at all. It was his bloody holiday time. He was running through beautiful woods. The last rays of the evening were painting the sky a deep, blood red. Soon it would be dark and he would return home under a blanket of stars. Tomorrow he had nothing to wake up for.

The woods were emptying. As Hugo jogged he heard the last cries of children leaving to go back to their homes. Another thing to be thankful for. He was always worried he would run into children from his school and whenever he thought a group of youths on the path ahead might know him, Hugo sped up, sprinting past them so quickly he hoped no one would be able to tell who he was.

Hearing about how his pupils had spotted 'The Beanstalk' out running was not something he looked forward to.

There was no danger of that at this hour, though, Hugo thought as he stopped and leaned against a tree, catching his breath. His t-shirt was stuck to his chest and there was a smell of damp about him. He stood panting for a moment then began to stretch out his calves. Hunger was creeping up on him and Hugo started to fantasise about what he would be having for dinner.

He needed to urinate and made his way through crackling bushes to the water and set about adding to the stream. He finished, tucked himself away, then turned to continue home. He hesitated for a moment, unsure of what he had seen beneath the foliage. He forced himself to look again. The heavy lower boughs of the trees dipped down into the water. The leaves, black in the failing light, brushed the surface of the stream. Hugo tried to convince himself the shoe sticking out from under these leaves was just a shoe. That it was a lone shoe, with no foot attached to it and no body waiting at the top of its leg.

Hugo crept closer, wading ankle deep into the stream. How peculiar. He was right. It was a body. There was no smell and he didn't feel scared or disgusted. Instead, Hugo felt overwhelmingly hungry, as if he hadn't eaten for a week.

He was intrigued by the body. Thinking this might finally be the exciting thing he'd been waiting to happen to him. Right at the beginning of the school holidays as well. If this was how things were starting, the possibilities for the next six week were endless!

Hugo reached the body and bent down and took hold of both feet. It was sideways across the bank and the head was submerged below the water. It looked to be the body of a young boy. Probably younger than ten. Hugo pulled on the legs in an attempt to pull the body free of the undergrowth. But something was holding it down and as Hugo pulled he wished again that he was able to build up some muscle. He wished he was strong. One day he'd find a way to pile on those thick slabs of muscle he saw on television and in magazines.

He gave a final pull and the body floated free. Hugo pulled it towards him and lifted the head from the water. He laughed when he saw the face. It was impossible. Impossible that he'd just been thinking about the little bastard and here he was, dead in his arms. There was a bruise on George Pearson's temple, but other than that, the body looked fine. Maybe fat little Georgie had fallen in and knocked himself out. Six or seven hours ago the little bastard had smashed an egg over Hugo's head. Now here he was, going white in the face with weeds caught in his hair. How the tables had turned.

The body didn't look particularly swollen, though, Hugo thought. He mustn't have been in the water for very long. People must be looking for him. His parents, perhaps…

Hugo scooped the body out of the water and ran up onto the bank. He held little George cradled in his arms. It was dark now. Even if people were looking for George (and who would be looking for the horrible little bastard?) they wouldn't find him in the dark. Hugo could feel his stomach rumbling, crying out for nourishment after his run. He had to decide quickly.

Hugo set off at a jog, the boy slumped over his shoulder. He licked his lips as he turned his plan over in his mind. Life was all about new experiences, and here was one delivered to him, almost on a plate. Something new that might finally bulk him up. Something that would help him build himself into a strong and respectable man. How ironic that little fat George would be the one to help him finally gain the other children's respect. Hugo was almost sad that no one else would ever appreciate the irony.

Today George had covered Hugo in flour and eggs but tonight Hugo would cover George in olive oil and garlic and maybe some rosemary. He'd have to explore what went best with this new ingredient. There was plenty of the boy to experiment with.

***

The next day, Hugo woke up earlier than he'd planned. He peered through the curtains at the silent street outside. It looked like a lovely day. Hugo swung out of bed, donned his running clothes, stretched, and set off towards the woods. After a while he came upon a gang of children he recognised from his class, looking about through the shrubs as though searching for a missing football. Or a friend.

They were huddled together, shouting "George! George!"

Hugo slowed down as he passed them, a smile on his face. He was looking forward to his breakfast.

A Holiday Gift

She handed me a gift as she stepped off the train today,
and said "Oh darling how I've missed you! Don't open it
until we're away"
I said "Me too!" and ripped it open at the station,
full of excitement and anticipation

What ever could it be? And my imagination ran wildly,
a hat, a scarf? But the texture was more like jelly
I looked at my gift and tried to think,
it looked back at me and gave a wink

It wasn't expected, but then neither was she,
this wife of mine, always playing tricks on me
I laughed and cried "Ha-ha very funny!"
But when I touched one it felt rather gummy

I felt a shiver and stopped where I stood
"Oh darling, I found them out in the wood"
It wasn't wine, shoes or cologne,
a bag of eyeballs is what she'd brought home

"Oh darling, thank you, what luck!
no, you shouldn't have, it's too much!
I've brought you a bouquet of flowers
and you've brought me a man, half devoured!"

"A woman," said she and I felt a shiver
It started in my stomach and crept past my liver,
"Anne helped me find them, isn't that a surprise?"
Anne was my secretary, with silky smooth thighs

"Yes I invited her along
What a lovely girl, I thought we could bond!
It was all going well, we had a terrific week,
the only problem was she talks in her sleep"

The station stood still and colours began to swirl
I looked around, where was this other girl?
"Anne stayed there?" I asked timidly
My wife smiled, shook her head and nodded at me

"She helped me find your gift, she's got such sharp eyes!
Sparkly and green like emeralds in disguise!"
I looked at the bag and Anne looked back at me,
I pictured her body buried under a tree

Slugs and flies in the hollows of her eyes,
all because I'd run mine up her thighs
I tried to calm myself and get a handle,
"Splendid my dear, we'll put them on the mantle!"

"Oh, splendid!" she said and my shoulder felt her head
We walked arm in arm and in my hand something dead
"I've missed you so much my dear little Fred,
next year, won't you come with me instead?"

Pad Thai

They had woken on the plateau every morning during the past week and Charlie would always rise first, when the grass was still wet, leaving her sleeping as he paced around the camp. There were six tents in total and each held two sleeping forms.

There was a wooden hut on the edge of the camp where their guides slept and cooked for them. Benches were set up outside and old dogs stretched around them in the early light. Charlie walked past the hut and away from the tents. He found a tree stump and sat down. The plateau was low and around it green hills rose steeply out of the jungle. Steam seeped through the foliage where the sun evaporated streams hidden beneath the deep green canopy. Already at this hour the sun was becoming unbearable and the birds moved lazily across the sky. Charlie sat with his bare back to the sun. He was tanned and had grown skinny from bowls of rice and tofu. A movement in the camp caused him to glance over. It was only a dog and he relaxed, knowing they would not find him for at least ten minutes more.

They had been in the jungle for a week and Thailand for three weeks before that. They were halfway through their first trip together, their first great adventure away from their families. Nine other girls and one other boy had had a similar idea, booking onto the same trip. They met in the Bangkok Royal on that first night, a big, excitable group beneath the bright lobby lights.

The girls couldn't get enough of them. "Charlie and Beth. Beth and Charlie. You're so good together."

The whole group had been good together other as they rushed out onto Koh San Road and surged into bars to drink

120

Sangsom buckets. They were at the start of their adventure under the neon lights, among the hustle and bustle of the pad Thai stand, the men offering 'ping-pong' shows and special excursions. They sat on a balcony with a seaside bucket of alcohol each. Charlie in the corner with Ben, a plumber somewhere in his early twenties.

"How did this happen?" Ben asked, biting his lip as he gestured towards Beth and a handful of the other girls by the bar. "We've got a month of this."

Charlie watched Beth twirl the umbrella in her drink between her fingers. She was laughing, oblivious to anything other than that moment. After this trip she wanted to go to Berlin and become an actress and Charlie knew she would do it.

"We won't forget this," Ben said, tapping his bucket against Charlie's.

A ripple of laugher carried them out into the streets and into tuk-tuks. They urged their drivers on, five people in each, racing through electric streets, the dark expanse of Thailand just beyond the street light's reach. They screeched up to a grubby building, paid their drivers, then piled inside to see a ping pong show, haggling with the owners for two free drinks per person. Charlie took Beth's hand and they took their seats among business men in suits and watched a talented girl open bottles and fire vegetables into the crowd from her vagina. A carrot landed in Ben's lap and he jumped backwards. Beth laughed into the table as Charlie swayed in his chair.

Hungover the next morning, Charlie and Beth took a boat trip along the Chao Phraya River. The muddy current carrying them to a riverside monastery where a child in an orange robe sold them bread to feed to the catfish swarming around the boat in a whirlpool of brown, curved bodies.

"Touch one, Charlie," she said, trailing her hand in the water. "They're so soft."

"I'd rather not."

She splashed water at him and he back at her as they continued down river.

They travelled around the country as a group, sticking to a loose itinerary outlined by the travel company. They went out as a gang and Charlie walked behind with Ben, as Beth walked ahead with the others. In a nightclub a Thai man danced with Beth and Charlie crossed the dance floor with his fists balled up.

"We're on *holiday*," Ben said, intercepting him.

Annie – one of the nine girls that made up their group – rolled her eyes. "Just let it be, Charlie. Christ. What's the harm?"

"Stay out of it, Annie," Charlie said, about to push past.

"Don't talk to her like that," Beth said, appearing beside them.

"Fine," Charlie said, feeling something twitch in his cheek. "Well, I'm going back to the hotel."

Beth reached for her drink. "Fine. I'll see you later."

He went back to their room and lay awake with the lights off. After an eternity of blackness, Beth entered, hot air following her inside. Charlie watched her from beneath a half-closed eyelid as she disappeared into the bathroom then re-emerged sans make up. He let out a sigh and stretched as if he were having a bad dream, but Beth either didn't notice or was too tired to pay attention to him. She climbed into bed, turned onto her side and fell asleep.

In the morning they loaded their belongings on to a coach and set off on a twelve hour trip north, towards the jungle.

"You were rude last night," Beth said as she passed Charlie on her way to a seat at the front of the coach.

Ben glanced at Charlie and shrugged, then moved across to let him sit down.

They ventured into the jungle dressed in boots, cargo shorts and light shirts. Beth stuck close to the Thai guide as they wound their way up a river bed under the light beginnings of the canopy. They walked for two hours, the jungle growing denser, buttress roots closing in around them, vines hanging head-high, birds echoing from somewhere overhead while flies harassed the slow, sweaty column of tourists.

Charlie caught up with Beth as she slapped at her neck and swore under her breath.

"Bastard flies," he offered.

Beth pulled her bag up on her shoulders and pushed ahead.

"Bad timing," Ben said, helping Charlie over a fallen trunk.

The heat was thick and fuzzy as they crossed a narrow stream, hot on the heels of their nimble guide.

This was days ago now, and as Charlie sat on his stump, waiting for the camp to wake up, nothing seemed to have changed. He looked out over the jungle again, then, giving in to the fact that he couldn't sit there all day, Charlie pulled on a t-shirt and headed in for breakfast. The guides emerged from their hut as he arrived, carrying trays of omelettes. Annie came over while it was being served up and Charlie stood up to offer her his seat.

"Cheers," she said, blowing on her plate as she sat down.

Beth, sitting nearby, seemed oblivious to Charlie's presence, let alone this calculated good deed.

After breakfast Ben cajoled her, Charlie and Annie into a trip to the waterfall cascading through the jungle below where they'd showered each day since arriving. They left in single file, heading down the hill through a field of tall grass before climbing over an old fence into a shade-filled meadow, where branches arched over the dark path, welcoming them back into the jungle.

Charlie and Ben walked ahead. They crossed a wide, shallow stream then hid behind a fallen tree, waiting for the girls to catch up. They jumped out as Beth and Annie were in the middle of the stream and Beth, caught off-guard, slipped and fell in the water. Charlie rushed to her but Beth swatted him away as she sat up holding her elbow. Annie helped her up instead, avoiding Charlie's eyes all the while.

They continued on in silence until the sounds of the waterfall met them through the trees. After sliding down a muddy bank, they stripped off to their underwear, the girls in bikinis. One by one they clambered up onto the thin ledge overlooking the shallow plunge pool below. They started to wash and Charlie edged his way along the ledge towards Ben.

A hand shot out and grabbed his arm, then Beth was saying, "Charlie! Be careful!"

Charlie pulled his arm free and silence returned.

Later, as the guides prepared the night's bonfire, Charlie decided to slip out of camp. Soon it would be dinner and he wanted to feel nothing but positive thoughts when he next saw Beth.

He walked quickly out of camp, passing behind the hut and down a muddy bank on the opposite side of the hill to the waterfall. There was no path here and Charlie slipped and skidded on his backside down the muddy slope. He stood up and laughed quietly, alone apart from the camp noises behind him. To the right was a gravel path leading back up to the tents; to the left, fields tapering off into the sloping hills that enclosed the plateau.

Charlie scanned the path for flowers but pickings were slim with only pale pink flowers growing in thorny bushes. He gathered them up regardless and after a while was scratched and itching but happy. Turning back to camp, he came across a large, muscular cow tethered in a field, the horns sharp and curved. Beside the cow was a single brilliant yellow flower, glowing as if having absorbed the brilliant colours from the surrounding flowers. Charlie approached cautiously. He was too young to die, but if Beth found his corpse clutching a bunch of flowers she would be forced to forgive him.

The cow looked sideways at him and Charlie smelled its warm, wet breath. Slowly, he reached out and snapped the flower from its stem. The cow jerked its head at the noise then settled again. Charlie was slowly backing away when the cow stamped a hoof and blew steam from its nose. Charlie turned and ran, scrambling over bushes and up the muddy slope to the camp, thorns dragging at his knees and wrists.

A guide playing solitaire in the hut winked at him as he appeared over the rim of the hill. "Flowers for me?"

Charlie tried to smile and made his way past the hut to the wood pile. The bonfire was in the process of being lit as he emerged, wilted flowers in hand.

Beth looked over and rushed to meet him. "I was worried. You're bleeding…"

"I'm OK. I'm sorry," he said, producing the ragged bouquet.

Beth swapped the flowers for a bowl of rice. "I saved you some food."

Later, they sat around the fire as a group, Beth nestled under Charlie's arm for warmth. Ben got up and when he came back he pressed a cold beer against Charlie's neck, dripping with water from the ice bucket. One by one the others left until there were just a few of them. Charlie got up and brought their sleeping bags from the tent and lay down next to Beth. The night sky was a wash of purple and blue, filled with thousands of milky stars.

"Beth," Charlie whispered, pointing above. But she was already asleep and soon he was sleeping beside her.

Kalopsia

Jack held the phone to his ear as the line buzzed softly, then died. He put the receiver down and stared first at the floor, then at the spaces between the framed photographs on the far wall. He sat there, on the edge of the bed, for a long while and even though he did not take his eyes off the wall, he could not have described a single detail of it.

After a time, he exhaled and ran a hand over his face; pinching his nose and puffing his cheeks out, letting the air slowly escape his mouth. Finally, he rose and searched about for his shoes. They were not by the door, nor were they beneath the desk. He found them half hidden under the bed, as though everything had become too much for them and they had tried to hide themselves away. Jack pushed his feet into them, slid into his jacket and walked out the door.

It was still raining when he stepped outside. The streets were blue and the sky was grey. There was nowhere he wanted to go, so he followed the rain downhill, heading east.

Jack had not smoked a cigarette in a long time. The first and only time he had bought a whole packet had been half a decade ago, at university, after a girl had ended what they had. He had bought a packet and then gone home and smoked them all, one after the other, and the smoke had drifted about the room, helping to unravel the knots in his mind.

There was a small shop just down the street from Jack's apartment and he went in now, a surplus of rain dashing in behind him. He joined the queue at the counter. A man in late-middle age, with silver hair and a long camel skin coat stood before him and it was all Jack could do not to turn around and walk back outside. The man's skin was tanned and short silver hairs lay softly against the skin like strands of silk. There was a smell of strong cologne. Traces of nutmeg and warm bark on a summer's day. The man's shoulders were damp with patches of rain water. Jack watched as he picked up a paper, folding it between his thumb and forefinger, before saying something to the cashier, slipping the paper inside his jacket and turning to leave.

When it was his turn to be served, Jack stepped up to the counter, and it was only with the third repetition that he heard what the cashier said.

"Cigarettes," Jack answered, without looking up.

His nails worked against the wooden counter and tiny splinters stuck into the tips of his fingers, minuscule baubles of blood shining on his fingernails. The cashier asked Jack another question and, after a moment, he handed over three times the right amount of money in change.

"Keep it," Jack said as the cashier called after him.

Jack stepped outside, and paused for a moment beneath the shop's awning, fumbling a cigarette into his mouth, the cellophane wrapper falling to the pavement. He stood there, beneath the patter of raindrops, and glanced up and down the street, but there was nothing there except the grey rain. He should get a dog, he thought. Dogs were good companions. Loyal. Dogs were always there, at your side, and you could walk along with a dog and be fine. What would Jack say if someone stopped him now and asked where he was going, and why he was out walking in the rain? He wouldn't be able to answer. There was nothing he would be able to tell them.

Jack held the cigarette between his lips, the filter damp with his saliva. He realised then that he had nothing to light it with, and cast about slowly for some inspiration, as though a flame might appear out of the ghostly sheets of rain. He squinted across the road. The far footpath was only just visible with the grey shapes of empty shop fronts, glass shining dully.

As Jack stared at the empty reflections, a girl emerged through a door beside a taxidermist's. Jack traced her movements as she paced slowly back and forth, before leaning back against the shop front, safely out of the rain. Her red raincoat throbbed through the grey drizzle as she lifted a thin cigarette to her mouth.

Jack pushed the hair out of his eyes. The cigarette slipped from his mouth and stuck to his wet lip. He crossed the street slowly, like a man wading across a river, the rainwater seeping through the holes in his shoes. When he reached the far side he pushed his hair out of his eyes again, then stepped up on to the pavement.

The girl looked up at him. She was tall and her blonde hair had been stained a dirty brown by the rain, like a favourite jumper dropped in a puddle. Jack stood before her without speaking, and felt the sun strain weakly against the back of his neck. The girl smiled and when this drowned boy said nothing in return, her smile slipped slightly, then returned with honesty.

Jack tried to smile back, but the anchor in his chest weighed him down. He put his hand to his mouth in some automatic gesture of embarrassment and was surprised to find the wet cigarette still held there.

"I don't think you'll have much luck with that one," the girl said, her words punctuated by dimples. "Take one of mine."

She reached inside her shirt pocket and passed the dry packet across to Jack.

"I... have my own," he said, patting his own pockets until he found the cigarettes inside his jacket. His shoulders were wet and he could feel the damp through his t-shirt. "Thank you, though," he said, his eyes caught on a freckle beneath the girl's left eye.

He shook out a cigarette, another identical little role of tobacco and paper. The girl held a lighter out, lighting it on her second attempt. Jack leaned into the flame and nicotine sank down into his lungs and smoke coiled up under his nose. He leaned his shoulder against the wall and closed his eyes. Smoke and the sound of water running through the gutters lit the darkness with flashes of pale blue.

"I'm Heather," the girl said.

Jack swallowed then inhaled deeply on the cigarette. He wanted to enjoy this, he wanted it to do him good, but the taste was bitter and the smoke made his throat feel like it had been scrubbed with wire. Still, it was a foreign experience, and there was pain in familiarity.

"Do you live near here?" the girl asked after a minute, glancing at him out of the corner of her eyes as rain rattled off the road then ran away down the hill.

Jack was about to answer, then he paused for a moment and said slowly, "No... I'm from somewhere else. My family live somewhere else."

It was not the answer he would have given earlier that afternoon, but now it was the right answer and it was good enough for the girl. She nodded in reply and Jack was glad to see her smile again. They smoked side by side in silence, Jack inhaling each breath of nicotine, the cigarette burning low and hot against his fingers and he dropped the remains of the cigarette suddenly, the orange glow hissing to nothing against the slick, grey streets.

The girl, Heather, drew her red raincoat around her, then turned to go back inside.

"It'd be nice to have a dog," Jack said suddenly.

Heather stepped back from the door and looked at him, her head tilted to one side, her freckles burning as though something had embarrassed her. Jack turned away, and then back to her. The moisture had been sucked from his mouth and dry balls of grey spittle coated his tongue. He swallowed quickly, but his throat hurt and it was not an easy action. He was about to speak, but laughed quietly instead, then turned his eyes back to the white mist of rain beating frantically against the road.

"I wish I had a dog as well," Heather said. Her hand fluttered to her mouth, bird-like, then dropped limply to her chest. "I just lost my cat... a dog would be nice. Something different."

Jack fumbled with the cigarette packet. Something warm and wet landed on the back of his hand and he wiped it away against his shirt. He offered the packet to her.

"Have another?" he asked, his eyes focused on the tip of her nose, lacking the strength to travel up to her eyes.

They each took another cigarette and Heather leaned in to light them.

Jack watched the smoke at the tip of his cigarette then said, with great difficulty, "You'd never be lonely with a dog."

Heather's fingers trembled as the rain lashed against them. They retreated back against the empty shop front. "It would be nice to have someone there when you came home at night," she said, her eyes on the far side of the world to where Jack stood, wrapped in his thin jacket, the shoulders soaked through, his chest marked by a dark, misshapen ring.

Jack nodded to the rain, but there was nothing more he could say.

Finally, their cigarettes exhausted, they turned to one another and smiled in farewell. Jack stood for a moment, nodded after the flash of red that was retreating back inside, then stepped out into the rain, heading back towards his own flat.

The rain continued throughout the night and the cigarettes slowly disappeared. Jack lay sweating with his arm wrapped around a pillow as yellow streetlight came through the window from outside. Strangely, he could think only of the girl. He wanted to think of the phone call, wanted to consider the words he had heard just that afternoon, think about what they would mean for the rest of his life, but the memory of the girl smoking in the rain smothered these thoughts, everything else sinking beneath the image of her eyes burning behind a cigarette.

In the months afterwards, it became engrained in Jack's daily routine to buy a packet of cigarettes and stand across from the taxidermist's, waiting. But the first time he saw her was the last and this grief slowly grew inside him and began to replace the old grief, until, eventually, the loss of both people settled in Jack's stomach and he thought only of the first, wearing the memory like a layer of skin, tucked away just beneath the surface. The girl was just an image he thought about sometimes when he went outside to smoke in the rain, wrapped in his father's jacket, breathing in the smell of nutmeg and warm bark on a summer's day.

Gulliver in Luiaard

The Missing Chapter of *Travels into Several Remote Nations of the World, in Four Parts. By Lemuel Gulliver, First a Surgeon, and then a Captain of Several Ships.*

Publisher's Note: In my capacity as Publisher, Friend, Cousin and Estate Agent I feel it necessary to share this new-found and captivating account of Captain Lemuel Gulliver's travels. In my duty of care as manager of Mr. Gulliver's *Redriff* estate I came across what appears to be a missing chapter, roughly fitting between Chapters X and XI of Part Three of Captain Gulliver's original manuscript. As Mr. Gulliver is at present unavailable to offer his guidance, I hereby publish said piece for the delight of the English public.

Richard Sympson

CHAP XI

After leaving the Royal Port of *Glanguenstald* I was to spend fifteen days at sea en route to the kingdom of *Japan*. During this time a most strange incident befell me. On the morning of the third day I awoke in my cabin to great cries from above and upon reaching the upper deck I was witness to an incredible sight. The ship's cabin boy had speared an almighty fish (it appeared to be some sort of giant tuna) and was in the process of wrestling with the beast to pull it from the ocean. Fearing the slight child would be pulled over, I rushed to his assistance. No sooner had I grasped hold of the spear, than the child and I were pulled into the perilous sea.

The child vanished beneath the water's foamy surface immediately and despite the crew's best efforts I was dragged out to sea at great speed by the mighty beast, the spear (which I gripped with all my strength) still lodged in its side.

After a short while I could hold on no longer and left myself to the mercy of the sea. I remember little else until I awoke to find myself upon a beach, and after a considerable amount of time required to compose myself, I ventured inland to see what strange country I now had the ill fortune to find myself upon.

I had not gone far when I came upon a town, very much in the style of the greatest cities of *England*, but considerably run down, as if neglected for many years. First thinking I had landed in *Norwich*, I soon realised my mistake and decided to explore further.

As I approached the citadel I was able to make out many balloon-like shapes floating above the buildings at differing heights, many with seemingly long capes hanging from them and some with what appeared to be people dangling from the bottom of these capes. I advanced as quickly as I could, eager to find out what these large shapes were.

Soon I entered the town to find it inhabited by people of seemingly European descent, the only difference between them and I was they appeared to be dressed in poorly made clothes and were mostly thin to the point of ill health, women, men and all.

I feared little for my safety, thinking myself amongst *Europeans,* and so carried on boldly into the city to try and satisfy my curiosity. I had not gone far before I came across a great crowd of people gathered around a man of extremely large girth dressed from head to toe in the finest embroidery any king of *England* has seen.

Assuming him to be the king of this strange land I immediately dropped to my knees, however, I was alone in doing so and soon stood back up.

A queer thing then took place. The large man began to

let out a slow and constant stream of gas from his rectum, accompanied by a noise that would be the delight of a small child. This is not so unusual in itself, but the effect was astonishing. As I watched, the man began to rise into the air, propelled by this gas as the audience applauded. Suddenly a second man, thinner and dressed in shabbier clothes, grasped the coattails of the great man and was borne into the air with him, to the delight of the audience.

The pair reached a great height and the ground below them was showered in coins from the pockets of the onlookers when sudden tragedy struck, and the second man lost his grip on the larger man's coat and fell to his death. I rushed towards the fallen man and took out various instruments from my surgeon's bag (which I have the good sense to keep about me at all times) and did my best to save him, but unfortunately he had perished.

Suddenly, I was taken hold of under each arm and lifted into the air by two more large men, who propelled themselves in the same manner of the first, expelling a stream of gas with an odour of roses.

I was taken to a fine building where two men of similar size and costume spoke to me rapidly in what appeared to be a dialect of *Dutch*. I understood easily enough and was shocked to find out their Eerste (roughly translated as 'Prime Minister', but one with total authority) was ill and near death. I was admitted into his presence and found his malady to be little more than trapped wind which I was able to expel, sending the Eerste up into the air for an entire hour.

Upon his return to the ground he thanked me by granting me an audience with him in which my curiosity about this strange land was to be resolved. We were on the island of *Luiaard* which was inhabited by many people who possessed the powers of gas propelled levitation. These people were held in great regard by the public and so naturally made up the upper classes, gaining their wealth from the donations of the poor who were greatly amused by the talents of their masters. As well as funding the lavish existences of these great men, the poor were also a source of amusement to them, the rich spending many hours levitating above their heads and watching like birds or flies as those below go about their daily business.

I asked why I in particular had been summoned to the Eerste and was told I was the only surgeon available. It appeared on this island that anyone with a trade or talent was seen as subversive as they may challenge the authority of the rich, foolishly believing they didn't deserve their status. These subversives were detained in a colony similar to the leper colonies of *India*. However, such was the gratitude that the Eerste felt for me that I was permitted to remain as his saviour.

He then asked me many questions about *England* and was surprised to learn we did not have our own equivalent of an Eerste. I told him we were sure to gain one as all the politicians of *Europe* were experts at discharging hot air. He enquired further as to the nature of my country and was surprised when I told him that the share of power was almost exactly the opposite in *England*, that as a matter of principle only those who proved themselves worthy were given positions of rank and that those who possessed a trade or talent were held in the highest regard.

He was surprised to learn that in *England* there were none who tried to gain power riding on the coattails of the successful, but instead all *Englishmen* were happy with their lot in life and lived their lives as fully as they could in the servitude of the Queen and their masters.

This greatly angered the Eerste and I was ordered to be expelled from his kingdom in the most ungainly fashion imaginable. I was lifted up and taken over the sea by the two guards who had brought me to the Eerste's home, then dropped into the depths of the water, where I floated for many hours before being rescued by Captain Defoe of *London*, a most respectable and honest trader who had the decency to transport me the remainder of my journey to *Japan*.

Mailer's Ghost

I wasn't quite sure why I had been invited to stay at Norman's house. I was to be there, alone, for a month and other than a cursory awareness, my knowledge of the late writer was lacking. Flying in from Boston under a bank of rolling white clouds I thumbed through a copy of *The Fight* and got a taste of Mailer as someone I should have been aware of a long time ago.

A taxi picked me up from the airport, out in the middle of the sand dunes, and took me to the house, the only brick mansion on a street of wooden houses facing out over the Provincetown bay. After setting my bags down I stood looking out over the grey waters, rumoured to be filled with sharks, and further out, huge whales.

Even with my limited preconceptions, there were things I didn't expect to find in Mailer's home. An attic study stuffed with hundreds of books on Hitler (research). The *Forrest Gump* soundtrack on cassette. The hallways decorated with flowery, mustard yellow wallpaper and lit by a selection of strategically placed lamps (courtesy of Mailer's late, final wife). The first weekend a storm rolled in off the Atlantic. I stayed inside, sitting by the large windows in Mailer's bar, sipping a beer as the waves crashed about in the 4pm darkness. During the empty nights I wandered about the large, silent rooms, wondering how I had ended up with free reign of Mailer's home for the entire month of November.

Gradually, I settled into a routine of rising at midday, cooking alone, reading for an hour, then trying to write terrible short stories about ex-lovers in Paris in Mailer's lounge, watched over by a photograph of Mailer with Gore

Vidal and Kurt Vonnegut.

It wasn't until the end of the week that I had my first unsettling experience. I'd finished off a short story the night before and awoke with the first hangover of the trip to the sounds of a voice calling up the stairs. I listened carefully, unsure whether the girl I had been dreaming about had spilled over into reality and was waiting for me in the kitchen. I climbed out of bed on delicate legs and completed a quick circuit of the house. I was alone.

In the dining room the large photograph of Mailer was hanging slightly lopsided. Arms crossed, hair grey, face scowling. He was trying to make contact, there was no doubt about it, wanting to rid his house of this British upstart who'd only found himself there by mistake.

After this first incident, I didn't hear from Norman for two weeks, but Provincetown in autumn is a place full of ghosts. Occasionally, I'd walk down to the town's bars, past wooden houses, every single one looking like the sort of place Ed Gein might have gone on holiday. The small American coastal town bars you see in films, with fishing nets hanging from the walls, dim lights and lonely men slouched at the bar, actually exist, and they're in Provincetown.

When I wasn't wandering the quiet winter streets I'd ride my bike around the sand dunes and when it rained I'd complete laps of Mailer's lounge, with the *Forest Gump* soundtrack blaring. It was on such a night that my second encounter with Mailer's ghost occurred. I had abandoned any hopes of writing something good and was in the process of heading upstairs in the dark, feeling along the yellow wallpaper as I went.

I managed to find the first light switch just as the *Forrest Gump* soundtrack slipped into *California Dreamin'*. The song flared up and a deafening cackle dragged me out of my skin, carried me to the top of the stairs, and slammed the bedroom door behind me. It was Norman, howling at me from beyond. I knelt beside the bed, promising him I would never ride my bike indoors again.

This seemed to appease Mailer, and we got along well for the final few days of the trip. It was not long before my last night came in the house, and after being turned out of the town's last bar, I invited a few of the locals back to see if we couldn't tempt Norman into making an appearance so that I could make peace with him, once and for all.

Around eight of us went back to the house and crowded around the dining room table. Norman's portrait smiled down at us, knowingly, as black waves sloshed against the shore outside. I found an old bust of Tutankhamen and we got to work on the whisky hidden inside. Once this was gone, we placed old Tut' in the centre of the table and linked our hands in the candle light. Solemnly and bathed in shadows, we tried for half an hour to contact Norman's spirit, chanting words none of us would remember, and could never repeat, as our shadows flickered across the bookcase.

Mailer was having none of it. He wasn't about to appear as entertainment to a group of drunken idiots who thought they could come and drink his whisky and dick about in his dining room. And, in all honesty, I was no longer sure I even wanted Mailer to appear. He was my ghost and I didn't want to share him. I was the one staying in his house, and why should the two of us provide anyone else with a good story to tell while propping up the bars of P-Town?

Norman knew what I was thinking and we decided he would stay out of sight that night. The others didn't seem to mind and they slowly drifted away from the table, one after the other, until it was just me and Norman's portrait, alone in the candlelight. I nodded at his portrait, then when the last guest had gone, I collected the empty bottles and slipped off to bed.

There was no ghostly wake-up call the next morning, but spirits of another kind were howling behind my head and jumping around on my queasy stomach. I lay in bed, glancing around the room, searching for something to help fight the hangover.

I was due to head home and would miss Norman's

house, but before I could leave, there was one thing I had to do. I pulled myself out of bed, slouched downstairs, stepped out onto the porch in my underwear, then swam out into the bay. My hangover began to drift away on the tide, and all was well with the world, until a thick rope of seaweed wound itself about my leg and began to pull me under. As the grey waters sloshed past my nose, I began to pray to Norman.

"Norman, we're friends!" I said. "I'm sorry we drank your Egyptian whisky. I'm sorry we disturbed you. I'm sorry I stole a pencil from your study and rode my bike around your lounge. I'm sorry!"

I was about to promise Mailer I'd dedicate my life to studying his works, when I realised I was able to stand up. I waded to the porch, brushing seaweed from my chest and spitting sand from my mouth. Just inside the doorway stood a table bristling with pictures of Mailer and his family. My favourite was Norman standing out on the porch, in summer, his stomach jutting out proudly over a small pair of blue trunks.

I stood staring at the picture as I caught my breath, Mailer grinning back at me. We were friends again. It might have been the water in my ears, but I was certain I could make out a faint whispering. Norman had enjoyed haunting me and, now it was my last day, he wanted to impart a great piece of wisdom to me.

I leaned closer and turned my ear towards the photograph.

"You fool," a distant voice whispered. "Get the hell out of my house, you fool."

And that's what I did.

Suspension

"I'm sorry, we're going to have to suspend you," she said
"It's all we can do until the decision comes down from Head
Office, I wish I could promise you'd be back soon"
He sighed, smiled and glanced around the room
but what about money, and what to do with his days?
He stood up, thanked them and left in a daze
no money for food, no money for drinks,
Suspended! Outcast! What would his friend's think?
Worries piled up, multiplied and became more,
than they should be as he stepped out the door
Outside it was sunny and there was a new record he wanted to buy,
He smiled, laughed, spread his arms, and began to fly

Just Another Winter's Tale

He stepped in from the cold, shabby in his battered red jacket. The bar hummed to a soft jingling tune and a few regulars mumbled along in conversation. A log fire roared in the corner. He shuffled across to warm his hands in the glow. A group of Inuits were playing darts and one roared as he hit a bull's-eye. Another picked up his glass and drained it in one go, before collapsing over a table, knocking a candle to the floor. Bull's-eye Inuit stomped it out.

The barman looked up at the noise, wiping his hands on his filthy apron. "Damn it you, goddamn Eskimos, keep it down."

Three of four fishermen looked up from their stools at the bar, chuckling to themselves.

"Oh God," the newcomer thought. "Not those guys."

He ran a hand through his scruffy beard. It was becoming frayed, and yellow was creeping into it ever since he'd started smoking again. His heart sank a bit more as he lit up another cigarette. That beard used to be his pride and joy.

The fishermen noticed him for the first time and shouted over.

"Hey hey! Look who's here!" laughed the lead fisherman in his woolly hat and checked shirt.

He tried to ignore them as he walked over to the bar. The fisherman's hat looked warm. He needed a new hat, ever since he sold his last one. He was going bald now because of the cold winds. Who would've thought it? Him. Bald!

"Hoho, welcome back, old buddy. You gonna be fighting those Eskimos again tonight?" said Fisherman

Number Two.

Fisherman Number One slapped him on the back as Fisherman Number Three called over to him. "Take it easy, man! Don't get too jolly tonight! Ha-ha!"

This sent them into fits and Fisherman Number Four fell off his chair to land on the damp floor.

The barman finished scratching his rear and came over. "What'll it be, Nick?"

"You got any sherry?" he asked hopefully.

The barman sighed. "You know I don't got any sherry. You drank it all up. And you best have some green for me, I ain't keeping you on credit this whole time, damn it!"

Nick pulled out his purse. A few coins rolled around in the bottom. "Look, man, Blitz said he can spot me, so it's OK, yeah?"

The barman put down the glass he was wiping and poured Nick a whisky. "Well, you make sure 'Blitz' does spot you. This has gone on way too long."

The barman noticed the rosy tinge creep into Nick's face as he poured the whisky and spat on the floor in disgust. "For God's sake, man! Sort yourself out. It makes my stomach churn to think what you used to be, and see what you've become: A broken down wino!"

He sighed and passed Nick the whisky. Nick drank it down and felt it warm him from the tips of his toes to the end of his nose. The barman poured him another then pushed a coin across the counter to him.

"Look, I know things are hard – my old missus ain't much better – but surely to God you can see why she's upset! It… well it wasn't natural. But that doesn't mean you can't fix it." He slid the coin into Nick's hand. "Go give her a call. Fix it!"

Fisherman Number Four called over. "That ain't gonna be any use. He's been naughty, not nice!"

The fishermen were off in hysterics again as they downed their shots.

The barman sighed. "Nick, just call her."

Nick looked at the coin in his old hand and slid it back

across the bar. "Barkeep, another drink."

The barman sighed and then picked up the bottle.

He had tried to call her. A month… two months ago, when everything went wrong. Called her up in the middle of the night. She sounded annoyed. Most people just weren't used to working all night. He held the receiver in his hand and leaned heavily on the payphone. He could see the snow whirling around in the blackness outside the bar. The Inuits roared behind him at some joke.

"Who is it?"

"Honey, it's me."

"You bastard, I'm hanging up!"

"No, no, no. Don't hang up, I want to talk to you. I'm sorry, I… I just want to come home is all, come home to you."

"Are you drunk?"

The phone swayed in front of him and his knees felt like giving out. "No, I swear I've cleaned up my act."

"My arse you have. Are you high? On that white powder?"

Nick wiped his nose. "No honey, I swear I'm not!"

It had been Him that had given Nick his first taste. He knew they were all doing it, round the back of the workshop, but he let it go on too long and then became part of it.

"Honey, listen I'm a role model, I…"

"Ha," she laughed. "You *were* a role model. What sort of Father are you though? You're certainly no saint."

"Honey." He could feel tears now. "Honey, I just want to be back with you. You can't have a Mrs without a Mr can you? Let me come home?"

"Never, *Kris*, never. I can understand why you'd want someone else. I really can. We've been together forever but why… I can't even say it, it's disgusting! Why not someone at work? A helper? I could almost forgive that, but this…"

And she had put the phone down. The snow outside seemed to have slowed. It whirled and twirled in slow motion, floating down to earth like Nick's heart gently

143

floating into his stomach.

Bull's-eye Inuit poked him on the shoulder then. "Hey, Nick are you done with the phone?"

And that's when he hit him, a quick left and then right and he was down. He could have been a boxer if he hadn't fallen into his old job. The fishermen laughed (One, Two, Three and Four) and then the Inuits piled in on top of him.

The barman handed him his whisky, snapping him out of his recollections.

"You know, I never understood. Why sherry?"

Nick drained the glass again and handed it back. "I don't know, either. I'm not sure I actually like the stuff to be honest. Just always seemed to be a lot of it around, you know?"

"Hmm, I suppose. So, are you still living with Blitz?"

Nick rubbed his red eyes. "No, things didn't work out. Got a place of my own, just off Pole Street."

The barman laughed. "Huh. Pole Street. So, you don't think Cupid is gonna come in and sort you out, then?"

Nick spilt whisky as he raised the glass to his mouth. The tremors were coming on again. He was feeling it. "Hey, you don't think you could help me out, man?"

The barman slammed his fist on the bar, causing the fishermen to look up. "God damn it, Nick! You need to kick that shit! I know you're down and out but it's your own goddamn fault. I mean who woulda thought, you and a… a…"

Nick wiped his hands on his red felt trousers, matted now with damp and dirt and covered in burn marks from cigarette ash. "All right, all right I know."

"You're not gonna get violent again are you?" the barman asked, eyeing the baseball bat he kept under the counter. "I don't want you to be fighting nobody again. Not them Eskimos or the Fishermen."

Nick sneered and spat on the floor. "Damn slanty-eyed bastards!" He made to get up but his legs failed him and he flopped back into his seat.

"Nick, you bastard! Leave them alone, they got more

144

right to be here than us! This is their ancestral land, their ancient hunting ground!"

Nick stared hard at a puddle on the bar. "I've been here just as long as them."

He leant forward and slurped up the stale alcohol off the surface, soaking his beard.

The barman winced then walked away. "Damn, Nick. Sort yourself out."

Nick was out of money. What now? Back to that little grotto of a flat? The little hovel he rented? He could hardly afford to pay gas and had to sleep curled up under an old sack on a damp mattress on the floor. His place was littered with takeaway tins and empty beer and Coca-Cola bottles. Even his toilet was broken. He had to piss in bottles and sometimes when he did in the middle of the night he'd wake up and the piss would've frozen. If he remembered, he emptied the bottles out the window onto the street.

Every day it was the same. Wake up at noon and sit around, drink a few beers and watch some cheap porn channels, then head to the bar. She was right not to take him back. He was disgusting. The shop he lived above used to be a toy shop, now it was a liquor store. Well, that was ironic. Goddamn yanks had taken over everything. Trying to buy out his business. It wasn't enough he had to deal with their screaming spoilt children? They had to follow him all the way up here and spoil his peace too? Coca-Cola on sale at every turn. Mocking him with their TV adverts and red lorries. Those bastards were the beginning of the end for him. Who were they to say what he could wear? Nothing was ever peaceful after that.

He was about to leave the bar when two middle-aged women walked in. A blonde and a brunette. They were both a little fat but Nick had had worse. One was showing a bit of leg. Great pins. Nick loved a strong hind leg. He stumbled out of his seat and held onto the bar. The women saw him and the blonde whispered something to the brunette and they turned and walked out the door. Nick sat down again and punched the bar. Shit. Messed that one up

145

again, Nick. He hadn't gotten laid since… since the last time, but he didn't want to think about that. The whisky was swimming in his stomach and he was almost sick. He needed another to settle it.

"Barkeep! Another!"

"No! Go home, Nick," the barman replied, the Fishermen laughing along. "Yeah go ho-ho-home!"

Just then the door swung open and they all ducked in; all eight of them, letting the cold air in behind them, snow dripping from their coats of fur to form wet puddles on the floor. There he was with his rosy nose, the flash bastard. He would've been nowhere if Nick hadn't given him a job. Stopped the bullying, when everyone used to laugh and call him names. Now he was taking over Nick's job. Well they said it's always the kids who were bullied that turn out to be arseholes. Sense of entitlement. Nick didn't owe the bastard anything. Even with that beautiful nose and those strong hairy legs.

All eight of them stopped laughing when they saw him and stood awkwardly pretending to talk amongst themselves. Of course he took charge. He was always good at that. The bastard.

"OK, Guys. Guys, go sit down. Prancer. Yoo-hoo, Prancer! Go and pull those tables together, get us some carrots." He looked at Nick with sad eyes and in the tone of one consoling a child said, "I'll just be a minute."

Nick looked away as he came and sat down next to him. He couldn't quite sit properly in the chair. He wasn't built for normal chairs, all eight of them struggled. Nick pretended not to notice.

"Nick." He touched his arm and Nick felt a shiver run through his spine as the thick soft hairs met his skin.

"Oh hi there. Didn't, erm, didn't see you come in."

"Well you know, just out for a drink with the boys. You know how hard we work. It's been non-stop in that workshop, it's so hard keeping all those little rascals in line!"

Nick stared into the bar.

"Oh I'm sorry, Nick. I forgot who I was speaking to. Of course you know what that's like. You used to. Well, you're looking good. I see you're still driving the sleigh eh? Ha-ha, oh the times we had! Well I best get back to the boys."

He rose to leave but Nick grabbed that silky arm and pulled him back down, almost making him lose his balance. "Listen you bastard. Don't come in here and act like this. It's your fault I'm here. You... you made me do things I didn't want to. Things between us! I mean I'm not even... I like people! Women! I'm married for Christ's sake!"

"*Were* married."

"Goddamn it! I am married and when she sees that it was just a mistake she'll take me back, soon enough. Everyone makes mistakes at the Christmas Party, don't they? I wasn't thinking, I was intoxicated. You made me intoxicated. I never touched drugs until then. Not even a few days before deadline day. Or when I had to drive all night. You think it was easy, up and down, up and down all night long. No one can do what I could."

"Kris, I understand you're angry but we all shared those nights with you... I was a good companion to you, you said so yourself..."

Nick interrupted, swinging his arm wildly and sending his empty glass crashing to the floor. "Don't call me 'Kris'! No one calls me Kris but her!"

Just then Blitz came over and the flash bastard got up to leave.

Nick held tightly to his arm, not quite wanting to let go and as he rose he fell on to all fours like an animal before scrambling upright again and sliding away across the wet floor. He sneered over his shoulder at Nick. "You're crazy darling. Unhinged!"

Blitz sat down next to him, shaking his head. "Don't let him get to you, Nick. We all know what an arsehole he is. Things haven't been the same without you at the workshop. The little men haven't got all the motivation they used to have. Course," he sighed, "it don't help them seeing you like this."

147

Nick didn't say anything so Blitz continued. "I'm sorry it didn't work out at our place, Nick. Like I said, I'm really grateful for all you've done for me, but it's just Bianca. You know, we really wanna make a go of it, have kids, all that. And, I mean I like to drink too – you know me – but it's just Bianca was a bit upset by that. She's not used to it."

Nick sneered. "Kids? How can you have kids with her? She's a…"

Blitz scowled. "She's a what, Nick? A what? An Inuit? Is that your problem?"

Nick raised his hands in surrender. "No, no, no, man. I don't care she's an Inuit, I mean she's one of the good ones right? I just meant aren't you incompatible 'cos, well, you know…"

Nick looked Blitz up and down.

"It doesn't matter that I'm different? We're living in a crazy time of progress, Nick. The doctor said maybe IVF, who knows? They can do incredible things these days."

Nick nodded. Incredible indeed.

The barman came over. "Blitzy baby! What can I get you? You gonna pay this schmuck's tab?"

Blitz sighed. "How much do I owe you?"

The barman scratched his stubble. "Well let me think… ought to be about thirty now, with tonight's as well."

Blitz pulled a wallet from somewhere and slid out a wad of bills. Nick raised his eyebrows. It looked like business was going well in his absence.

Blitz struggled to peel off the notes he needed. "Little help here, Barkeep? I'm not made for this."

The barman reached over and peeled off a ten and a twenty. "Oh sorry, Blitz, I forgot. I'll send a few pitchers over for you and the boys, erm you guys."

Blitz got up to leave. "Appreciate it."

Nick ran a hand over his balding head and touched Blitz on the arm. "Blitz, you couldn't spot me a ten?"

Blitz looked at him with eyes full of pity and put his furry appendage on Nick's shoulder. "Go home, Nick. Go home, get some sleep."

Nick stood up and almost fell over. "Go home? You bastard, after all I did for you." He brushed Blitz's arm from his shoulder. "Get your damn stinking hoof off me, you animal!"

Blitz backed away. "OK, Nick. OK."

The barman had the bat in his hand. "Nick, get out."

Nick tried to protest. "But…"

"Get. Out. Old man." The barman patted his open palm with the bat.

"OK, OK. I'm gone."

The wind hit him head-on when he opened the door. It bit into his face, worse than any Inuit punch. He staggered out into it in his black boots. They were wearing out in the soles and his stockings were getting wet. He'd sold the gold buckles and his gold belt buckle for beer money long ago.

Nick vomited into the snow as the door closed behind him. The snow melted in a puddle around the brown mincemeat mess. There was some carrot in there. Strange, he couldn't remember eating carrot. He straightened up and stared back at the bar. He could hear those bastards singing in there and he shouted into the wind.

"You better watch out! You better beware!" and then he stumbled over and fell flat in the snow.

He pulled himself up and made his way over to where his sleigh was parked. There was no use brushing the snow off himself. He was already covered in all sorts of crap. He used to have the finest velvet suits. The kids would all tell him, sitting on his knee, how soft his suit was. He'd sold all of them now, except the one he wore. But he'd never sell that sleigh. It appeared out of the darkness like a mirage as he ploughed through the snow. That beautiful golden sleigh with its red velvet seats and spacious luggage compartment. The two donkeys he had reined to the front were looking a bit worse for wear. Their matted fur seemed frozen but they shifted their weight from hoof to hoof every now and then to show they were still alive.

Nick climbed into the sleigh and picked up the reins. Something was poking into his back. He fished around amongst the empty sacks and pulled out a half empty bottle of sherry. Things were looking up. He could start again. He took a swing from the bottle and cracked the reins.

"Ho!"

The sleigh set off slowly and the bells began to ring. Nick took another hit of the sherry and cracked the reins again. Soon they were flying along the snow, both donkeys straining under the weight of the sleigh. Neither the donkeys nor their passenger saw the red lorry appear out of the darkness until it was upon them.

***

At the bar the Fishermen laughed and the Inuits played darts in the homely glow of the fire. The gang of eight sat around the table laughing about Nick and their days pulling the sleigh, Dancer saying, "Well, he was all right really."

The barman wiped out a glass and placed it upside down to dry on the bar. Poor Old Nick. He'd fallen a long way.

Then the door burst open and the Coca-Cola delivery man was blown in with the snow. Everyone looked up, seeing the wild look in his eyes as he shouted over the roar of the blizzard outside.

"Everyone come quick, I've just hit something! This old fat guy in a sleigh just came out of nowhere. I think... I think I killed him!"

A screeching, animalistic wail came from somewhere as seven reindeer fell to the floor in tears and Rudolph ran out into the snow.

Restaurant Story

The door opened and another couple stood awkwardly, not knowing whether to wait or whether to sit themselves down. Outside the rain hung in the air and the street lights burned blurry-orange through the night-time fog. Henry heard the door creak open over the noise of the restaurant and saw the couple out of the corner of one eye. They hadn't moved and were trying to catching his attention.

Henry ignored them, focusing on the table setting he was straightening. The knife was at one o'clock, when it should have been at twelve. The hands of Henry's own watch showed ten, as they had when he had started that morning.

Unable to ignore the new couple any longer, he left his table setting with a sigh and went across to greet them. There was a script, rehearsed a hundred times a day, which fell from Henry's mouth without effort or consciousness. When he had said it the first time the customers found themselves with drinks, after the second time they had their first course, and so on and so forth until they left with either smiles or flat nods with Henry standing by the doors, asking them to return soon – a request as empty as the rest of the performance.

He sat the couple down and went off to fetch their drinks: an Appletiser and a Bloody Mary.

There was a noise of protest from the kitchen as Henry relayed the food order. More new food in an endless stream of food. People would always be hungry and even if they were satisfied today, there was always tomorrow. A chef's job was never done, even when the restaurant was closing. From amidst the piles of dirty cloths, pulled-out units and half swept floors, Nico appeared, a paper chef's hat falling over one eye.

"Henry," he said. "This is last table. Kitchen closed, yes?"

Henry wiped a hand across his mouth. A yawn escaped between his fingers. "Fine by me," he said, after the yawn had subsided.

He took the food across to the new table and the script slipped from his lips and then he left them to their meal. He ran both hands through his hair. Afterwards there was a layer of grease on his fingertips. There was an itch on his chest that had been bothering him all day, but nothing he had done had been able to cure it. His neck was sore where the collar of his shirt rubbed at it and his top button made swallowing painful. Before he could undo that button and take off the shirt to scratch his chest there was cutlery to be polished, tables to be set, customers to be served, bins to be emptied, floors to be swept and maybe leftovers from the kitchen to be eaten.

When there were leftovers at the end of the night, Henry ate them out of a sense of duty, rather than any feeling of hunger. Always, he felt that he deserved some treat after his shift, and the fact he derived no pleasure from the cold burgers or chicken breasts did not stop him hoping for them.

The second-to-last couple asked for the bill and, after a minor dispute about the husband's carbonara, left the restaurant, smiling and calling thanks. Henry mumbled a few half words and noises in the general key of gratitude. The couple disappeared into the rain. As the door was about to close behind them, a woman ran from the street and wedged herself in. Henry pulled the door open and the woman hid an embarrassed smile as she came inside. Henry looked over the restaurant. There wasn't too much to do. One table would make no difference.

"Table for one?" he asked and the woman nodded.

Henry led her to an empty table as she shook water from her hair and shoulders.

"Is this all right?" Henry asked, going through the

script.

"Yes, thank you," the woman said. She looked quickly about the restaurant. "I'm just going to go to the toilet, is it OK if I leave my bag here?" she asked, holding up a rain soaked backpack.

"That's fine," Henry said. He watched the woman cross the restaurant to the bathroom She was tall, thin and maybe in her late twenties and she shivered slightly as she walked.

"One more table, Nico," Henry said through the kitchen window.

"Kitchen is closed!" Nico repeated, leaning on a sweeping brush.

"Just one more," Henry said.

"OK, OK. One more fucking table, even though I tell you kitchen is closed."

"Thanks, Nico."

"OK, OK. Hurry up," Nico said, waving him away.

When the woman returned from the bathroom Henry went over. She was wearing a vest top, her wet jacket discarded on the seat beside her. She scratched distractedly at her arm as Henry tried to take her drinks order. Her eyes darted about the restaurant as though looking for someone and Henry almost turned around to see who was behind him.

"Sorry?" the woman said.

"Oh, can I get you a drink?"

She was an attractive woman, Henry noticed now, tall but perhaps overly thin for him. Her clavicle protruded from her chest and there was little muscle to her arms.

"I'd like a drink," she said, as though this was something she had just realised. "Yes, I would."

Henry waited for her to continue. "Erm, what can I get you?"

"Oh," she said and scratched her head. "I think I'll have… a coke."

Henry brought the drink and the last couple left the restaurant. The end was in sight. Suddenly Henry hungry.

"Nico, any food left?" he asked through the kitchen window.

"Maybe Henry, fucking maybe. You let me finish and go home. No dessert for that table, too."

Henry returned to polishing his cutlery, looking up every now and then, watching the woman slowly eat her cheeseburger. It was the same cheeseburger hundreds of people had eaten that week. There was nothing special about it; it was about as standard as a cheeseburger could be, but this woman seemed to be savouring it as though it was the best food she'd ever had.

"Is everything all right here?" Henry asked, back on script.

The woman held the burger halfway to her mouth as though caught in the act of sneaking food from the cupboard as a child.

"Yes, it's fine," she said. Her shoulders relaxed. She smiled. "It's really good actually."

This was not the throwaway smile Henry normally encountered in customers, or gave out himself. Slightly thrown off, he left her again and went about the business of clearing up the restaurant.

Nico appeared from the kitchen, dressed in his own clothes. "Henry, maybe pint of Stella?" he asked.

Henry poured him the drink.

After a while Nico finished his drink and left. Henry went over to clear the plates away from the woman. She had finished everything and sat back as though satisfied after a Christmas dinner, or sex.

"Was everything all right there?" Henry asked, the script falling from tired lips.

"Yes," she said.

Henry took her plates to the kitchen and returned with the bill. The woman paid in silence and Henry wasn't sure if it was just because he was tired that he couldn't think of anything to say. The woman gathered her things.

"Goodbye, goodnight," Henry said and the woman nodded shyly.

Before opening the door, she turned around at the last second and spoke. "I just wanted to say thank you. I... I have trouble with eating, with anorexia, and this is the first meal I've had on my own in a long time, so thank you for looking after me."

Henry had lost the script and searched around for something to replace it.

"I'm... I'm pleased. I'm glad, that you had a good time," he said.

The woman smiled and then she pushed through the door and out into the night. Henry sat at the bar. There wasn't much to do now. The door opened and a man and a woman came blustering out of the rain. Henry glanced over at them.

"We're closed," he said, turning his attention back to his cutlery.

A Nice Trip

The metro rattled onwards through the tunnels of Paris. Jack wiped sleep from his eyes and shook his head. Across the carriage an old man was playing the accordion. The tune was suitably Parisian. Jack turned to the black tunnels passing by outside, glancing at red and green blurs of graffiti that no one would ever read. A sign on the door said, in French, English and Spanish, to keep your hands inside the carriage at all time. A cartoon rabbit was shown, his hand trapped in the door. *Un lapin*, Jack thought.

The train hissed to a halt. A few people swayed with the rhythm, their elbows and shoulders bumping into the person next to them. The accordion player was making his way down the carriage, rattling a plastic cup.

Jack was about to dig through his pocket for some change when a robotic female voice echoed through the train. "Palais Royal, Musée du Louvre."

Jack sprung up from his seat and pushed past the accordion player. It was his stop. He stood for a moment on the platform. Paris had always had a certain smell, he thought. It was not a smell he could explain, but he knew there was something that he breathed in that made his heart hammer against his ribcage.

The crowd moved up the steps and Jack found himself in the jostle for the exit barriers. He looked up, automatically, and there she was, waiting at the bottom of the steps that led out to the street. Then he was through the barrier and beside her, his bag swinging awkwardly against the back of his knees.

"I've brought you a sandwich," she said, thrusting a brown paper bag towards him. "It's beef. You like beef don't you?" she asked as they moved together up the steps and out into the sunlight.

"Yes," he said, holding a hand up to shade his eyes against the light.

They were in a wide square now; with a road on either side and the Louvre to their right. They made their way across the square as boys on roller skates wound around them and jumped over lengths of pipe, balanced atop piles of bricks. A man had a bucket full of soapy water and a tennis racquet with no string in it that he was using to blow giant bubbles across the square.

Sally eyed Jack's sandwich. "There's no lettuce though. I know you don't like lettuce," she said."

"I do," Jack said, trying to unwrap the sandwich with one hand while holding his bag in place with the other.

"You never used to," she said.

Less than a minute later they were at her flat. The red door opened with a click and they stepped through into the midday gloom seeping in around the edges of the blind. The flat was a studio with only one main room and a tiny bathroom and a smaller kitchen off to the left.

"I didn't make the bed," she said, looking around as though searching for some hidden clutter.

"I thought you might want to sleep a bit. We've got until tomorrow morning, and I'm already off work so we can do what we want," she said, sitting down on the edge of the unmade bed.

Jack put his bag down and kicked off his shoes.

"Thanks, Sally," he said quietly, putting the untouched sandwich down on the bedside table.

Sally moved over to the other side of the bed and slid beneath the covers. Slowly, Jack got in beside her, keeping his clothes on.

"I'm really tired, I got up at four am," Jack said as he lay beside her.

"I bet."

They lay there awkwardly, like strangers.

Jack slid down beneath the covers until his head was

level with Sally's on the pillow.

"Thanks for inviting me," he said.

"I've missed you," she said in her own, old voice.

"I missed you too."

Jack focused on the topography of her face. He tried to find something familiar there, but his memories were blurry like washed-out photographs. There was something familiar about being beside her, though, and he felt the heat rise to his cheeks. He inched towards her, not daring to touch her. Sally's eyes widened and her lips parted as though in surprise, but she did not move away.

"Thanks for inviting me," Jack said again.

"It's OK," Sally said.

Jack kissed her on the lips then quickly pulled away.

"I'm glad to be back in Paris," Jack said as Sally's arm slid around his waist and pulled him towards her.

A sudden vibration, like a bird tapping at the window, split the room. Jack pulled away and rolled on to his back.

"You'd better get that," he said, his imagination going into overdrive at the thought of who could be calling.

"It's fine," Sally said.

"Get it," Jack said

She leaned across him and checked her phone then lay back beside him.

Jack smiled at her to buy himself some time to think of something to say.

"Hmm," she said, the noise like a hungry cat.

"What are you 'hmming' about?" Jack asked.

She shrugged and he pulled her towards him. Afterwards they lay together, closer now, and nothing seemed to exist beyond the edges of the bed.

Jack curled Sally's hair around a finger. "Has it always been this colour?" he asked.

"You know I used to dye it."

He couldn't remember.

For a few minutes they lay in silence. Sally's phone rang again and she leaned over and put it on silent.

"Answer it if you want to," Jack said. "I've come here

and intruded in your life, so don't think you've got to change for me."

"It's not him," Sally said.

Jack nodded.

"It's not. Anyway, I think we should get up. We can't stay in bed all day."

Sally swung her legs out of bed and began to dress. She raised the blind and sunlight flew into the room. Jack squinted, watching as Sally made her way about the room, searching for something.

"That was nice. Just now," she said. "I think… I feel like we shouldn't do it again, though."

Jack was about to reply but realised he wasn't sure what to say.

"It's not fair, on… him," she said. "We're not together, but it still feels like I'm cheating."

Jack had thought about this for a long time, over the past months. Perhaps strange situations were just part of growing up.

"Hey," she said, relaxed again, her hand on his shoulder. "Don't be sad, tomorrow we'll be in Nice."

"I'm not sad," he told them both.

***

The Eiffel Tower lay below, like a pin in the map of Paris. He had seen it enough times already, and turned from the window. The plane was almost empty but still they were crammed together by the window. In the air, in-between destinations, they were neither living her life in Paris, or their old life back home. Here there were no rules and as Sally leaned her head on his shoulder, they both imagined that the changes of the past year had not taken place.

After a while, Sally dozed. Jack stroked her sun-warmed hair and felt happy, for a moment, at least.

The plane landed, they found their bags and soon they were on the bus into town. They travelled along the Promenade des Anglais, staring out through the windows.

Sally pointed to the leather-clad motorcyclists outside the window. "I saw a man get hit once, when I was younger," she said, absentmindedly.

"He was doing tricks and fell off and was hit by the car behind."

"Jesus," Jack said.

"He died, of course," Sally said.

The bus stopped and they got off.

"Here it is; my grandparent's apartment," Sally said as she led them through a gate, up to an old wooden door.

She keyed in a combination and they stepped through into the gloomy lobby. It was cool inside, but stuffy with still air. The walls were tiled in deep green and the wide staircase was of dark wood.

They creaked up to the apartment, Sally's forgotten memories flooding back as they went.

"Oh my God!" she exclaimed suddenly.

"What?" Jack said, glancing about.

'I just remembered,' Sally began. "That door there," she said, pointing to a dark wooden entrance, set back from the first floor landing in deep shadows. "My grandmother always used to say a witch lived there and one day, we saw her, my brothers and I, and we all ran screaming out of here."

"You didn't tell me you were bringing me to a haunted house."

Sally pushed his chest. "You'll be OK."

The apartment was on the third floor and Sally spent a good twenty minutes taking Jack from room to room, pointing out paintings and furniture by famous artists and designers whom her grandparents had known in their early days in Paris.

"This is amazing," Jack said, casting his eyes over the lounge. A desk stood by the window, looking out to sea, paper and pen at the ready. "My grandparents had a caravan."

They unpacked their things in the bedroom where Sally had stayed as a child. There were two twin beds and they

160

pushed these together so they could sleep next to each other.

"This will be OK," Sally said.

"Yeah, it'll be fine," Jack said.

When they had settled in, they packed for the beach and headed out. Couples walked along the promenade, children ran, and cyclists weaved in and out of joggers.

They found a spot on the beach and spread their towels.

"I need to work on my tan," Sally said, taking off her bikini top and spreading oil over her chest.

Jack tried not to look at the sweaty, fleshy mounds. "I thought you didn't like using oil," he said. "You used to be scared of cancer."

Sally lay with her eyes closed. "It'll help me tan."

Later, Sally pulled him from his book and they splashed into the sea. Jack dived under the waves and emerged shivering. Coloured rings of tanning oil floated on the water. Sally was a good swimmer and she bobbed along, eternally ahead with Jack swimming after her.

They returned to the apartment and lay on the sofas as the sun set outside. The sofas were at a right angle, and they lay with their heads touching. As darkness crept into the room, Jack turned onto his side and moved his head closer to Sally's.

Her eyes met his.

"Let's go out for some food," she said.

***

They spent four days in Nice, in total, and each day passed much like the first with picnics on the beach and evening walks along the seafront. Each night they went to sleep holding hands, but it was impossible to hold each other over the chasm between the mattresses and so, as soon as they each felt the grip of sleep, they would turn their backs to the other and take ownership of their own bed.

On the third day, after lunch, Sally stood and slipped on a t-shirt.

"I think I'm going to go to the shop," she said, sliding

her feet into her sandals.

'OK,' Jack said, his eyes on the phone in her hand.

On returning Sally passed Jack a selection of chocolate bars.

"I've brought you some chocolate. I know you love it," she smiled as she sat down.

"Thanks," Jack said. But opening the bag of Maltesers, he felt like a child on holiday with his mother.

Later, Sally rubbed the last of the oil into her chest, hoping to make the most of this final day of sunbathing.

"I was dreaming..." she began, but stopped as though changing her mind.

Jack propped himself up on one elbow. "You were dreaming?"

"I was dreaming, last night that we were in bed together."

"It was good," she added.

Jack laughed, wincing slightly at what he was about to say. "It doesn't have to be a dream."

Sally smiled, opened her eyes to look at him, then went to sleep.

***

That evening, they dressed in their best clothes and walked down the promenade, past the Hotel Negresco towards the market. It was their last night and they ordered seafood paella and wine. Jack insisted he use the last of his money to pay for it. The food was fantastic and the wine better. After a few glasses Jack threw caution to the wind, basking in his temporary victory.

"What does he think of you being here with me?" he asked.

"I told him," Sally said, taking a sip of wine. "He said he hopes we have a good time."

Very mature of him, Jack thought and then he forgot about him and turned his attention back to his meal.

After the plates had been cleared away, they sat across

from each other, sipping the last of the wine. A few tables down a group of Spaniards on holiday laughed and the sound carried down to them like the warm wash of the tide.

"I've had a really good time here," Sally said, the white fairy lights above their table reflected in her eyes.

"So have I."

"I was thinking," Sally began, "as it's the last night... we could..." She was unable to finish and her eyes darted to the table cloth.

Jack nodded. "I'd like that. But first, we have to get ice-cream," He nodded to a kiosk across the square selling ninety-nine different flavours.

They walked back along the promenade, beneath the bright dusting of stars, eating the finest ice-cream in existence. At one point Sally seemed to hurry ahead and as Jack languished behind, he swore he saw the glow of a phone in her hand. Never mind, he thought. They were here together, in that moment, and everything else that existed outside of that could not touch them there.

Back at the apartment they fell into each other's arms. The two beds pushed together were awkward and in the end they stayed on Sally's. Countless memories of old times were enclosed in that singular act and Jack tried to recapture them all at once, wanting to re-experience every aspect. He thought of the ice creams and wanting to try all ninety-nine flavours at once, in case he never tasted ice-cream again.

It was less spectacular than the first time and afterwards Jack hopped awkwardly back on to his own bed. They lay that way for a while in the darkness. After a few moments Sally spoke.

"Why do all men like that?" she asked.

Something jumped in Jack's stomach.

"Who else have you done that with?" he asked, afraid of the answer.

"Well..." she said his name, and then, quickly, "It's not a big deal."

Jack felt sick. He rose from the bed and stumbled down the hallway. The wine was swimming in his head. He locked himself in the bathroom and punched the blue-tiled wall. It felt as though some of his knuckles were broken and he bit his lip and swore beneath his breath as he paced about in his underwear.

He felt like the pain in his hand had woken him up and he looked around the room, wondering what he was doing there. He wondered why he had come and he wondered why she had told him what she just had. He had known deep down that the whole trip would be a mistake, and so, he imagined, had she.

There was a faint rapping at the door, accompanied by Sally's voice.

"Come back to bed."

Jack didn't answer. He wasn't ready to go back. He was angry, furious, but it was nothing she had done wrong. She could do what she wanted with whomever she wanted and it was no business of his. The mistake had been their seeing each other again.

Eventually he opened the door.

"I'm sorry," she said and he accepted her apologies, guiltily.

In the morning, they made their way about the apartment, collecting up their things. Jack stood, alone, in the kitchen, cutting thick slices of bread and spreading them with jam. His hand still hurt and the memory of the previous night was not a pleasant one. He put the bread onto a plate and was about to carry it through to Sally when he felt her arms around his waist. He put the plate down and turned to face her.

"I love you," she said, her voice breaking.

"I love you, too," Jack said, and for a minute they stood in their embrace, their tears mingling on each other's cheeks.

***

The plane journey was the reverse of the trip from Paris. They started out close together, in each other's arms, but as the reality of Paris approached they drifted further apart so that by the time Jack spotted the inky curve of the Seine and the white bubble of the Sacré -Coeur, they were both engrossed in their books.

After the airport they did not go back to Sally's apartment. Instead, they wandered around Paris. Towards dusk, they found themselves at the Place de la Concorde.

"I wonder what all of these flags are for?" Sally asked, pointing to flags of countries that hung from Concorde all along the Champs Élysées.

"I'm not sure," Jack said.

"My grandmother said Obama is visiting this week, it could be because of that," Sally said as they passed the Obelisk, heading towards the Champs Élysées.

Jack looked at the date on his watch. "It's D-day," he said, "June sixth. That'll be why the flags are there."

"Maybe," Sally said distractedly. She checked her watch. "I have to go to work. You can get the metro from Concorde to the airport; leave plenty of time, won't you?"

"I know. I will," Jack said.

Something was vibrating in Sally's bag.

"You need at least an hour to check-in."

The buzzing continued.

"I know. Go to work," Jack said. "Thanks for the holiday." He felt tears spring to his eyes. He wiped them away and when they hugged he felt her phone vibrating against him, through the bag.

"Go to work," he said again, attempting to hold his smile.

"OK," Sally said. "Safe flight. Speak soon."

"Speak soon," Jack said.

Then she walked away, getting smaller and smaller as she moved down the Champs Élysées. Jack walked in the other direction. He passed the Obelisk, leaving the Eiffel Tower and Arc de Triomphe behind him, and then went down into the darkness of the metro.

Glass Flowers

A few miles outside of town the land washed away into a wide, flat expanse of fields, dissected by a single, narrow road which led down towards the river bank. At the end of the road stood a small village, the road connecting town and village like an umbilical cord. In winter the sky here was the colour of charcoal, and in summer the sky turned a hot, reluctant blue. The village was not alone in this flat expanse. Another village of similar size sat on the far side of the river. These two villages had peered at each other for three generations, one on the east bank with the town at its back, and the other on the west, with open countryside behind it.

A bridge spanned the river and on the east side was a small wharf where the ships that had found their way along the river from the North Sea spilled their cargo. The people of both villages had grown up with the sounds of these cargos rushing and crashing on to the dock day and night and had long since become deaf to the sounds of the wharf.

Something else no one paid any attention to was the great green pile of broken glass that had gathered in the small yard between the wharf and the bridge. It had begun as a small pile, hiding under the shadow of the bridge where weeds and graffiti made a den for teenagers, before being slowly added to over the years. The glass was the green of old ball gowns or emeralds and it glinted with quick, white flashes in the sunlight and at night it seemed to spread slowly across the small yard, growing like it was alive.

When Lindsay Cotton had committed suicide off the bridge, the glass heap was not yet there. Its predecessor had been a smaller pile of pig iron, temporarily occupying the yard on its way to be smelted in the furnaces of the nearby town. It was with these twisted lumps of metal that Lindsay filled her pockets, hoping they would drag her down to touch the sludge that made up the riverbed.

George Chandler's desperation had carried him to the bridge that night, running up from the west village just as Lindsay climbed up on to the railing and stood looking down into the water, her hair rushing about her face in the wind. Although Lindsay and George were from opposite sides of the river, there was no sense of Montagues and Capulets about their affair and if their families had known they wouldn't have cared, even with the baby.

There were no cars on the bridge that night and the moon shone on the water and the heaped pig iron sat under the dull yellow lights of the wharf. George had run up to Lindsay with his lungs burning and words gasping between his teeth. It was only when he touched Lindsay's elbow that she became aware of his presence, and the shock nearly sent her tumbling down into the water.

"Lindsay, don't do it, please. For the love of God, don't do it," George said.

"It's all I can do," Lindsay answered, her eyes black with resignation.

"I can look after you both, I promise. I'll do anything..." George said, trying to climb up beside her.

"Working the furnaces for the rest of your life isn't enough," Lindsay said, her eyes flickering towards George as her hand brushed her stomach.

"I'll do anything. I'll work two jobs... I'll..."

Lindsay turned her head slowly towards George, the wind howling through the iron bridge making her movements sound like those of a marionette.

"Please..." George had said softly, his cheeks wet, the image of Lindsay a kaleidoscopic distortion.

Lindsay shook her head slowly. The black water was only a short drop below. When the truck came rattling over the bridge in a flash of headlights, she stepped out into the night and dropped silently down to the water.

George threw himself against the metal barrier, but his hands were clamped tight against the flaking paint and he couldn't bring himself to jump in after her. He watched Lindsay fall for a long time, her dress billowing up around her like a flower in bloom. Then, with a burst of white spray, she disappeared beneath the water, and the pig iron in her pockets carried her down to the bottom of the river.

George Chandler had stayed there until the black sky became broken with grey. For a long time he did not cry. It was only when the sun broke behind him that he forced himself away and walked back across the bridge. He had only gone two steps when he collapsed to the ground. It was in this state that the postman found him, two hours later.

Lindsay's family tied flowers to the bridge each July, and occasionally George would visit in the middle of the night and stare out over the water.

It wasn't until many years later that George began to avoid the bridge, taking his children up into the town via winding back roads. The journey would take an hour longer, but despite their complaints, he refused to tell them why he would not cross the bridge. Only his wife, sitting silently beside him with her arms folded, knew the reason.

Eventually, the Cottons moved away, leaving no one to leave flowers by the railing. It was then that the great pile of jewelled glass appeared, and every day it seemed to grow a little bit larger, shimmering in the sunlight like a mirage.

One Last Drink

He was leaving Antigua today. He had loved its picturesque streets and lazy sunny days and to leave now seemed too soon. He was having one last drink in the hostel bar. He needed it. He had spoken to her on the phone that morning. Things were going great, she was having fun. What business was it of his if she was out with guys? They weren't together anymore. And she was tired of talking about how perfect it'd be when he returned.

When he had first left to come here the pain had been a constant pounding. He'd missed her every day. He missed her in the way people miss each other in books and films. The way he'd thought had been a terrible exaggeration until the day he left. Two months later the constant pounding had died down to a persistent dull thud.

His Mojito was good. He remembered another Mojito with her in another bar thousands of miles away. Now she was in bars thousands of miles away with guys that were thousands of miles away from him. Before he went to sleep each night a part of him wondered if things could ever be the same again.

The bus driver came in and called him. The bus was early. He hadn't finished his drink.

'¿Solamente soy yo hoy?' he asked the driver.

'Si, es solamente usted'.

The bus set off through the sunny streets. He looked out through the window and said goodbye.

Milk, One Sugar

He came into the room struggling with the tea. Hot liquid sloshed from one of the mugs and he quickly side-stepped to avoid burning his leg. The tea landed on his jeans anyway and the material soaked to a darker blue. The girl looked up from the bed and took one of the mugs before he'd offered it.

She took a sip. "I told you to put cold water in it."

"It'll cool down," the boy said.

He set his drink on the table beside the bed and sat down beside her.

"It'll cool down quicker if you do what I say," the girl said.

The boy took a drink of his tea. It was too hot and he blew air on to his burnt lip.

"Have you found anything?"

The girl sat up straight, reaching for the travel brochure. "Ecuador. It's exactly far enough away. If we went any further away we'd be coming back on ourselves."

The boy smiled. "How much?"

"We'd have enough if we got jobs now and worked for about four months."

The boy scratched his head. Outside it was dark and lights from the steelworks lit the snow on the window ledge. He stood up, closed the curtains, then sat back down on the bed.

"It's exactly what I need," the girl said.

She held up the magazine, the pages falling open on a picture of an ancient tortoise on a beach of white sand.

"I suppose so."

"You can do it, babe. A few more double shifts, cut back

on a few things, and we'll be out of here." She squeezed his hand, her eyes tracing the shapes of the tortoise's shell.

"OK," the boy said. "Let's do it."

***

"Sit down," the boy's mother said as he came into the kitchen.

A half-empty bottle of wine stood on the table and half a cigarette burned in the ash tray. The boy sat down. The lights were turned down low and outside street lights glowed against the sky.

"Where is he?" he asked.

"Out." His mother picked up the cigarette and put it between her lips. "We... I need to talk to you about something."

The boy slid his chair back and leaned his chin forward on the table. "Getting divorced?"

"Don't roll your eyes. We're not getting divorced." She stubbed out the cigarette and took a drink of the wine. "They're making cutbacks. Your father's been let go, so we'll need you to help out around here for a few months."

The boy thought of white beaches and tortoises. There was a bitter taste in his mouth. "What do you mean?"

"I mean what I just said."

"I'm leaving. Ecuador. A few months."

His mother reached for the packet, then lit another cigarette. "There's nothing we can do. You'll have to think of something else. Go to Egypt another time."

The boy noticed a splinter in his thumb. He sucked it out and spat it on the floor, blood shining on his nail.

"Don't spit," his mother said. She crossed to the window and stood smoking, looking out into the night.

***

It was raining outside and his own reflection was all he could see. He took a deep breath and turned back to the room.

"When were you going to fucking tell me?"

"She only died a week ago," the girl said, spinning in the desk chair. "I didn't kill the old bitch, did I?"

The boy picked up one of her teddy bears from the bed. He played with the loose flap of its ear then threw it down. "Just wait. I can come too. No one's about to leave me fifteen grand, but I've been putting some aside."

"How much?" she asked, her back to him now.

"Enough."

"How much?"

The boy turned back to the window. "Why do you have to leave in two fucking weeks? You know I can't afford to come now."

"I can't wait for you forever. I'm nearly nineteen. I need to start living my life." She spun around in the chair to face him. "I'm sorry. Maybe if you'd worked a little bit harder you could have come as well."

The boy punched the wall and his knuckles sank into the plasterboard. The bedroom door swung open and the girl's father came into the room.

"It's time to go."

"I'm sorry. I'll be one minute," the boy said.

"Son. It's time to go."

***

He watched them from the cafe across the road from the station. Her father pulling her rucksack out of the car boot, bending under the weight. Her mother holding her by the cheeks, both of them crying. As he nursed his tea he thought he saw her look about for something, but he couldn't be sure.

The train eased into the station and the trio gathered close for one last family hug. She stepped aboard. Again, he thought he saw her look about and then the train began to pull away and then it had left the station and was gone.

The boy watched the family drive away and then he sat watching the trains come and go under a sky the colour of slate. After a while his watch told him it was time for work. He stood up and left, his tea cold and untouched.

So You Think You're Hot Shit?

Percy had been in New York for two days. New York City, New York State, the United States of America. The Big Apple. The city that never sleeps. Percy himself had hardly slept. It had been a whirlwind tour and he'd spent the past two days trying to visit everywhere he'd seen in Scorsese and Spike Lee films. He didn't know if he'd succeeded in finding any of the actual locations, but to him, the whole place looked like a film set with its skyscrapers and wide boulevards with steam rising from sewer grates.

He was there because, rather unexpectedly, a popular magazine had given him a prize for writing, then flown him all the way across the Atlantic for an awards ceremony, which had taken place the previous night. The event had been in a swanky hotel off Central Park and he'd met a famous golfer there and brushed elbows with the odd literary giant. It was about time he was getting recognition, Percy thought. He was twenty-seven and had published three books, each of which failed to arouse the critics. Now he was getting somewhere. This could be his moment.

Now, on the third and final morning in New York City, New York, U.S.A, Percy found himself wandering around Lower Manhattan. Where he was exactly, he could not say, but if any of his friends back home asked him he would have made up some street name. He'd seen a comedy show off Broadway on his first night and thought that sounded glamorous. 'Off Broadway'. Glamorous but casual.

He made his way along this Lower Manhattan street, caught in the throng of New York life. Everyone was busy, bustling along the sidewalk, mobile phones glued to the sides of their faces. Percy stared after every yellow cab that passed him and stopped for a moment beside a construction site. Men in orange vests and yellow hats were busy digging up chunks of earth, yelling at each other over the din of car horns and the clatter of feet on pavement.

Percy checked his watch. It was 10.32 am, which left about two hours before he needed to head to the airport. There was a diner across the street that looked like a good place to rest up.

He lugged his suitcase through the door then stood back as a man with a bicycle helmet under his arm pushed past and went out. The cafe was almost as busy as the street. The aroma of frying eggs, bacon and hot grease was thick in the air and Percy felt his stomach rumble as he pushed his way through to the counter. Behind it, big men in greasy aprons moved about, shouting orders and handing food across to hungry customers. Somewhere, a radio hummed out a steady stream of jazz.

Percy could make neither head nor tail of the menu. He did not know what 'grits' or 'biscuits' were, and before he really had time to decide what he wanted, a fat greasy man appeared on the other side of the counter and shouted, "Yes?"

"Yes," Percy said. "I mean, I'll take a burger… cheeseburger and fries. Please."

The man nodded and held his hand out. Percy pulled a $20 bill from his pocket and handed it across. The man went off and a minute later came back with Percy's food in a plastic tray. There was no change. Percy stood for a minute at the counter. Every time he tried to raise the burger to his mouth he felt an elbow in his ribs. He decided to scuttle off and find a table.

He sat down at an empty spot near the door. An old guy at the next table lowered a paper and looked at him. Percy turned to his food. He held up one of the pale, limp fries, thinking he could almost see through it. The man at the next table rattled his paper, then folded it up and laid it down on the table top. Percy took an uncomfortable bite of his rubbery burger and tried to ignore the man.

175

"So," the stranger said.

Percy gulped down his fires.

"So," the man said again.

Percy felt he had no choice but to smile politely and acknowledge him.

"You think you're hot shit, do you?" the man asked as he raised his coffee to his lips.

"Sorry?" Percy spluttered, a lump of dead cow caught in his throat like cardboard.

The man wore a fedora and he pushed it back on his head and raised his eyebrows. "Didn't you hear me kid? I said 'So you think you're hot shit, do you?'"

Percy swallowed painfully. "No... I don't think I'm... I don't think I'm 'hot shit' at all... Sorry do I know you?"

The man shook his head. "Why would you?"

Percy didn't know why. The guy was probably in his early sixties. He was thin and wore a pinstriped three-piece suit. He looked a lot like a photograph of William Burroughs that Percy had once seen, but he didn't want to ask this guy if he was a dead writer, known for his heroin addiction. Instead, all he said was, "I don't know why I'd know you. Do you know me?"

The man sighed, blew out a slow stream of air through his teeth and shuffled closer to Percy. "Look, pal. You're hot shit now. Welcome to the world of celebrity. This is how it feels!"

Percy stared at the man. He could not remember seeing his blood-shot eyes or sallow cheeks, peppered with grey stubble, the night before. It was possible though, that this man had been at the awards ceremony and had seen him there.

He decided modesty was the best policy. "Oh, I don't know if I'm famous. It certainly was an honour to win an award for doing something you love but, still..."

The old man shook his head, saying nothing.

Just as Percy was about to speak again, the man held up a hand. "I'm pulling your winkie, kid," he said, rubbing his eyes with his thumbs. "I've seen your picture. In a magazine. Bet you think that makes you hot shit?"

"No," Percy said.

"I bet you think the world is yours now. All you gotta do is send a letter off to whoever you wanna work for and you've got the job. Hey welcome aboard! I bet you think the world will spread her legs and let you dive right in and f..."

Just then the door banged open and two cops came shuffling in, yelling their order to the guy behind the counter before they'd even sat down. A woman at the counter stood up and hurried out, her eyes glued to the floor.

"I'm sorry?" Percy said, turning back to the man.

"You really aren't going to go far if you're deaf too," the man said.

Percy decided to ignore him and turned back to his meal. In the time the man had been speaking to him, his fries had wilted and shrivelled up like slugs in salt and the burger had dried to a grey mulch. Percy abandoned his food and turned back to the man.

"Who knows how far I'll go? I won an award and I'm grateful for that. Who knows?" He took hold of his suitcase and rose to leave. "It's been nice meeting you."

"Sit down," the man said. He pulled out a packet of cigarettes, tapped one out and inserted it between his narrow lips.

Percy paused, his knees half bent for a moment, then sat back down again. The man pulled out a match, snapped it into life and offered the flame to his cigarette. He took a few puffs and blue smoke seeped into the air around his head, then he flicked the match away across the diner.

"I'm not sure you can smoke in here," Percy said, glancing at the cops. They had laid their hats on the counter and were busy upending a bottle of syrup over bacon and pancakes.

"People will always tell you there are things you can't do," the man said, the tip of his cigarette glowing orange. "They gave me an award once. They gave me an award and told me I was at the top of my game, but what does it matter if this guy says you're shit hot, if the next guy's never heard of you?" He took his cigarette from his mouth and stared at it a minute. "Plus," he continued as if a spark of inspiration had just floated up from the tip of the cigarette and landed on his nose, "maybe the second guy doesn't even like the first guy. Maybe he doesn't want to give you a job out of hatred for this other asshole. Then it won't matter who you are or how good you think you are."

Percy shifted his weight from one bum cheek to the other. "Hmmm. I suppose."

A waitress appeared and bent down to refill the man's coffee cup. "Anything I can do for you, hun?" she asked, smiling her crooked white teeth at Percy.

"I'm OK, thank you," Percy said and the waitress shuffled off, on her never ending mission of refilling coffee cups.

"You can forget about that," the man said, tracing Percy's gaze. "How do you expect to get the women if you can't make a success of yourself?"

"I didn't become a writer to get girls. I did it for the love of..."

"The love of words? Of language? Literature? For the pursuit of a higher meaning? Some universal truth? Bullshit. Some men spend their whole lives chasing accolades and fame, some don't, but there's only one reason a man does anything in this life, and that's to get women," the man said, dropping his cigarette into his mug of fresh coffee.

Percy stared at the coffee for a moment. The cigarette was turning yellow as it sank into the liquid. He checked his watch. He really had to be going.

"Well?" the man asked.

"Well, I should be going. I have a flight..." Percy said, starting to stand up.

"No, I mean, what do you think, do you have an opinion? You do everything for women? A piece of ass?"

The question was so ridiculous that Percy had to laugh. "No. You really can't know me if that's what you think," he said, sitting down again.

"You're not a fag are you?" the man asked.

178

"No I'm not," Percy said. "And what if I was?"

The man said nothing.

"I've got to catch a flight," Percy said.

He rose and dragged his suitcase from under the table.

"Good luck, kid," the man said. "I'm sure I'll never hear of you again."

Percy put the suitcase down and turned back to the man. "What makes you think that?"

"You got something lined up for when you get home? Job offers coming in? People clamouring to buy up all your little stories?"

"Well," Percy said as he dragged the suitcase towards the door.

"See you on the slush pile," the man shouted, reaching over to scoop up Percy's discarded food.

Percy swung the door open and paused in the doorway. The smell of smog and the clatter of traffic met him. He took a last look back into the diner. A young girl, beautiful and blonde, had just sat down in his newly-vacated seat, beside the old man. She brushed a few strands of hair behind her ears and took the lid off a plastic bowl of soup.

The man put down Percy's burger and turned to the girl.

"Soup," he said.

The girl ignored him as she brought her spoon to her lips and blew gently on the red liquid. The man took a sip of his coffee and Percy's stomach turned as he spotted the soggy cigarette floating against the man's nose. The man lowered the cup and looked at the girl again.

"So, you think you're hot shit," he began. "I saw you in a magazine. I bet you think you're hot shit!" the man was saying in the direction of the girl.

Just then, the two cops barged into Percy, still dawdling in the doorway.

"Come on, move it along there!" they shouted as they shoved him hard in the chest. He moved to let them past then quickly turned back to hear the girl's response.

"Shut up," she said simply, her attention on her soup.

The old man fell silent. He brought the coffee to his lips

and drained off the remainder in one go. Then he stood up and walked towards the door. The girl ate her soup. Percy stood open mouthed, and then the old man shoved him out into the street. Percy hesitated then walked after him. He'd taken two steps when his suitcase fell open and his possessions blew away down the streets of Lower Manhattan, New York City, New York State, U.S.A.

Fantastic Books
Great Authors

CROOKED
CAT

Meet our authors and discover our exciting range:

- Gripping Thrillers
- Cosy Mysteries
- Romantic Chick-Lit
- Fascinating Historicals
- Exciting Fantasy
- Young Adult and Children's Adventures

Visit us at:
www.crookedcatpublishing.com

Join us on facebook:
www.facebook.com/crookedcatpublishing

Printed in Great Britain
by Amazon